HOW TO SAY "I LOVE YOU"

An Olive Street Series Novel

AMANDA SCHEIRER

COPYRIGHT

DEDICATION

This book is dedicated to women around the world and especially to the wonderful women who have inspired me throughout my life. May we always be brave enough to follow our dreams no matter where they could lead, strong enough to trust our instincts, and free enough to allow our hearts connect to one another.

ACKNOWLEDGMENTS

This book is ten years in the making. It began as a play I starting writing while in undergrad. Three years ago that play saw its first production, but I always knew there was more to the story than I could put on the stage. That is when I set out to create, How to Say " I Love You" the novel. Now I've seen this story grow and flourish into the upcoming Olive Street Series.

I am so thankful for the love and support I've received along this journey. I especially have to thank my parents for their unwavering support. They've always been there to nudge me forward and remind me I can accomplish anything. My inner circle, my friends, who've been an incredibly gracious focus group and my most spirited cheerleaders. And to the man I swear I wrote into existence, for holding my hand along the way.

Finally, thank you for reading.

PROLOGUE
RED STRING OF FATE

T he first time I saw him, I was six years old. His name was George Anthony. I'm sure I must have seen him before that, but that is the first time I can remember. It was the first time he registered. My heart was much more advanced than my brain could possibly have been. I saw him. The man I love. The one I would love for the rest of my life. But, not just be in love with him. No, cursed to love him forever without him ever knowing.

George Anthony was my neighbor's youngest son. Well, he is their youngest son. He is still their son, but neither of us still live in our childhood homes next to each other. Two steps out my back door; three garden stones, a step down into the alley, metal gate, a step up out of the alley and two more steps to his back door. Growing up in the inner city, that was all that separated us. Our whole city block was basically one large, slightly dysfunctional extended family. It seemed as if the dangerous reality of our city didn't exist for our row of homes. On Olive Street everyone knew each other and took care of each other. I was raised spending as much time in George's mother's kitchen as I did my own. It is that comfort of having family all around and running barefoot from house to house, that is the thing I think I miss the most about my childhood.

It was cold out that night when I first saw him. It was mid-December in eastern Pennsylvania so it was more than cold, it was absolutely frigid out. I know because my mom was smoking out the window of our second-floor sun porch. The sun porch was a narrow room just wider than a hallway that ran the length of the second floor. It connected the three modest bedrooms and bathroom up there. She only did this when it was too cold to smoke outside because there was a strict no smoking in the house policy for the Reilly's due to my asthma. She would sit in the dark, her legs crossed on top of our homemade toy box. She looked like a fairy sitting atop a mushroom in a dark forest. I can probably count the number of times I saw her there on my two hands, but that image of her is forever engrained in my brain. There was something otherworldly about her, something mystical. She always told me we came from the gypsies, that my great grandmother could place a hex on you with just one look. Her powers were supposedly passed down to my grandmother, my mother and finally me. Although, I still haven't seen any recognizable or worthwhile abilities manifest themselves. Silently sitting, watching the Christmas lights sparkle that night, I snuck up on my mom. I always wanted to be near her. Fear of missing out was far from being a catchphrase in the early nineties, but I very much suffered from it. Wherever she was, I wanted to be. I silently crawled up on the toy box facing her and pressed my forehead against the cool window to watch the lights with her. I stared out, smiling at the lights against the dark blue, nearly black sky. But then I looked down to the ground below and there he stood. Just outside his kitchen door, he was standing there silently smoking a cigarette and staring off into the alley behind our houses. He had no idea that we could see him from the second-floor window. We sat completely in the dark, but he was illuminated by the motion security light his father installed just that week. The harsh white light cast a surprisingly warm glow on him. I examined him, unabashedly staring in a way that you can only get away with when you are young. My mother must have noticed me observing him, but there is no way she could have known what I was thinking, feeling or where it would lead. The first thing I noticed was his skin. His permanently tan skin was so different from my pale, pasty skin. His face was shaven smooth except for where it gave way to the short coffee-colored hair of his sideburns. It was combed forward in a George Clooney-esque Caesar cut. He was tall, but not intimidatingly so. His striking presence came from his broad shoulders. I got the feeling that I wanted to know what it would be like to have his arms wrapped around me. He was older by quite a few years, twelve to be exact. A fact that wouldn't even come into my consciousness for several years. Even still, somehow standing with one hand inside of his Temple University hoodie he made my heart swell. He was mysterious to me, he was intriguing. There was a twinkle in his eye as he stared out at the thin layer of snow on the ground. I was stuck still at that moment and I thought in my teeny tiny mind "I love him."

Preposterous! I know it is. Thinking back on it now, it seems insane. How could I possibly fall in love at six years old? I didn't. I couldn't possibly have even known what love meant. Honestly though, all these years later I don't think I am any more enlightened on the subject. But nevertheless, that singular night is how this whole story started. It began twenty some years ago between row homes; apartment buildings, tiny yards, back alleys and the Greek Orthodox church down the street. In the middle of the biggest city in Pennsylvania and among families who'd been in their houses for generations. We grew up in a place where the bond between neighbors could take on any sort of familial relationship.

Our lives seemed magnetized to each other, naturally intertwined as though we were connected by some mystic power. There were times when I was younger I could never have imagined my life without him in it. Even as we both grew up and away, he always seemed to know when to float back into town, setting my head and heart to spinning. Fated, I thought. Destined, I said. Tied together by the red string of fate, I read.

During my freshman year of college, I took an Asian Cultures class as a part of my general education courses. One night I was up well past one in the morning working on assignments for a few different classes. I was sitting against the wall of windows that looked out over the quad so that I could watch the wind blow through the trees when I needed a break. After finishing forty pages on Carl Jung and his archetypes I moved onto my last reading for the night. It was so innocuous. Read pages fifty-two through seventy-five of a book on Chinese mythology. As the clock drew closer to two in the morning and the wind howled through the trees, I read a passage in that book that would shake me to my core. I re-read it three times that night and twice the next day just to make sure I understood what it was telling me. The red string of fate is a myth that occurs in many Asian cultures, but it originated in Chinese culture. It is believed that everyone on earth is connected to another person. They are fated to be in their lives in spite of everything that might keep them apart. This is because the love deity, the matchmaker god has tied these two people together with the red string of fate. It is tied to each of their ankles and it lasts through time and space to bring these two people together when the time is right for them to find each other. Some stories include the lovers meeting as children and then again as adults, other stories had them never meeting, but perhaps passing each other on the street every day for years without noticing one another until one day...bang! They meet and it is all over from there. My stomach flipped with each sentence I read because it spoke so deeply to me. George and I are connected by the red string of fate. We are supposed to be in each other's lives and we will be together eventually because the string tied around my ankle leads directly to his.

Nevertheless, it has been seven years since that late and windy night in the library. It has also been seven years since the last time I have seen George's face or heard his unmistakable laugh. I have never given up on the belief that the red string of fate would ultimately bring us together. But every year grows even harder than the last, as I feel a piece of myself is missing. It is like an aching phantom limb.

Seven years I thought about him and dreamed about him, but life kept us apart. Seven years... that is, until last week.

CHAPTER 1
CHOOSE LIFE

Oh my god, what is he doing home? What is he doing home midday on a Tuesday? The crack of the metal door startled me. My heart is pounding in my chest. Shouldn't he be at work doing something very important that no one could possibly know about? Maybe he won't see me. I slowly, stealthily pull the book I'm reading up so close to my face that I can feel my breath bouncing back at me. *Gross.* Well, I guess I would rather have him think I'm extraordinarily short-sighted than have him find me with no make-up, a huge zit that came to visit my face this morning and my hair greasy from the conditioning mask I've left on for far too long. At least the need for glasses is cute and can easily transition into a sexy librarian type of fantasy. There are no redeeming qualities to sweatpants and poor hygiene. I try to quiet my breathing. I don't want anything to draw his attention. Silence. Good. I think it just may be working. Now, all I have to do is just wait it out until he goes back inside his house. Then I can scurry into mine, take a shower, put on a full face of make-up and my most alluring, but casual outfit. It should take me roughly all day.

"Nessa!" His voice forces me to inhale violently.

Shit, shit, shit. He saw me. There is no hiding now, I've been spotted. I want to look up and see him. Jesus, I'd stare at him until my eyes dried up and fell out of my skull if given half the chance. Just not right now, not in this moment. I don't want this to be the image of me that he has in his head. This was supposed to be my safe space, my own little corner. No one should be able to see me on this little chair in the back corner of the yard. No one except my next-door neighbors. He is supposed to be working. He is not supposed to be standing five feet from me on the day I decide to fully transition into a slug.

"Nessa! Hey!"

I can't ignore him and honestly, I don't want to. I look up and my heart sinks all the way down my body and into my butt. He looks gorgeous leaning against the chain link fence ever so nonchalantly. His hazel eyes shining in the sun call me to him. I am no longer in control. I can't feel my body. It is like I'm floating across my tiny yard right over to him. I feel awkward and self-conscious by my appearance, but his smile is so welcoming that I begin to buzz with adrenaline. Now, I'm standing only inches from him and his hands reach out to my face. He isn't afraid of my zit or repulsed by my pudge or blotchy, pale skin. He doesn't gawk at my sweatpants or recoil from my greasy hair. He is not sickened by me at all. No, in fact, he is looking at me quite dreamily. Holding my face in his firm hands, he whispers in my ear, "Welcome to London." *London?* What does he mean, London? I try to look around, but my head is still in his hands and I can tell he has no plans of releasing me. He leans into me and ever so gently touches his lips to mine. I have been waiting for this moment for as long as I can remember. It is so tender I could cry, but then it doesn't stop and I can't breathe. I panic and try to pull away. I try to breathe. I gasp for air and...

I'm awake...and breathing thankfully. Eyes bulging open in fear, it takes me a moment to recognize where I am. All of the adrenaline that had been coursing through my body is now all collected into a softball sized pit inside my stomach. I am staring up at a beige ceiling inside of a beige room with the bright orange of a Trainspotting poster assaulting the periphery vision of my right eye. I can recite the movie mantra by heart. "Choose your future. Choose life." *Choose, eh?* Lately, every time I see that damn poster I feel like it is mocking me. I want to close my eyes and go back to the dream, but I am afraid. So, I lay still peering out through barely opened eyes. I can't shake the feeling of the dream even as I come face to face with the harsh light of reality. I tilt my head slightly to the right, to the poster so rudely intruding on my sight. "Choose your future..." Choose your future. I turn back to the ceiling, but my eyes are going cross-eyed just laying here looking at nothing. So, I turn them ever so slightly to the left and this pit in my stomach grows exponentially. Danny is sleeping so soundly, so still. He sleeps in a way that I never could, as if he had no thoughts in his head to keep him up at night. He is peaceful and handsome and sleeping next to me. It is infuriating. I, on the other hand, sleep like a meerkat or at least what I imagine a meerkat, sleeps like. It takes me forever to settle down. I am constantly popping up in the middle of the night. I toss and turn and then when I wake up midmorning, I have permanent dark circles around my eyes. My fury subsides as I examine him, taking in every inch of his face. It was his soft features that drew me to him when we first met. He looked like he jumped off of a Disney animator's drawing table. Round, gray, puppy dog eyes with soft, full lips and a gently curved nose. He has the most welcoming face of anyone I know. I could make a home in his cheeks. The night I met him I immediately wanted to tell him all my secrets. Spill my soul to the kind stranger at the bar. I could have too and he would've taken them to his grave.

It was an unusually quiet Thursday night at The Temple Bar and I was working my usual closing shift. I wasn't exactly thrilled with the turnout. There was a table of girls in the back corner, two regulars at the bar and a group of college kids playing darts in the back. It always quieted down the week after graduation around here, but this was dead. Knowing I wouldn't be walking away with fists full of cash I was happy enough to work on my writing behind the bar. I placed my green, multi-subject notebook on the bar, slid up on the mini fridge and leaned over to start. Stray strawberry hairs fall around my face as the open space in my black V-neck tee shirt fills to capacity. I feel smart, sexy and powerful. I pick up where I left off.

It had been the longest winter Larissa Summers could remember in her whole life. The unrelenting snow had turned New York City from a wonderland into a bleak, gray prison. The glare of neon lights burned her eyes as she walked past the row of Chinese takeout places below her apartment. She was starving but couldn't stop into any of them for some shrimp fried rice.

"You're gonna break that!" A gruff voice from behind me interrupts my thoughts.

I look behind to see Ralph hanging over the pass.

"You're gonna break that refrigerator!" He points at my butt.

I shake my head. "Number one, rude. Number two, it's fine. I've seen Greg put a keg on top of here before."

"Mmmhmmm....sure Red, whatever you say." He turns back into the kitchen and bangs some metal bowls around.

After months of rejecting Ralph's advances and invitations

to dinner, he had given up on "charming" me and taken to simply picking on me at any turn.

No. There would be no delicious dinner for Larissa tonight or any night soon. It would only be fifty cent ramen packs for breakfast, lunch, and dinner. You see she spent every spare dollar she had on the dress...and the shoes. The dress and the shoes that were sure to stop him dead in his tracks at the fundraiser. She was determined to win Chance Elliot even if she had to go on a hunger strike all week to do it.

"You should write me into your stories." Ralph's grating voice pierced my progress once again.

I don't even bother to look back at him. "Why on earth would I do that?"

"You're writing one of those lady porn books, right? Your readers will love a former porn star turned Michelin star chef. Very sexy." His confidence would be laughable if it weren't so misplaced.

"Ralph you are none of those things." I glare back at him.

"Yea, that's what you think, Red. You don't know me. You don't know nothing." And then, back into the depths of the kitchen he walks, banging plates this time.

I press my pen back down on to the paper and push back a stray strand of hair with my left hand.

Then he walked into the bar. I didn't think much of him at first. It looked like a normal family of four coming in, a mom, dad and two boys. Just another distraction from my writing. They took a seat at a high-top table right in front of the bar, so, I closed up my notebook and made my way over with some menus. All four greeted me with friendly hellos.

"Hello, Dollface." The father began.

It was the kind of greeting that immediately made the hair on my neck stand up, but I kept my smile on. Even though I hated being called doll, the patriarch had a distinctively Italian charm like Robert DeNiro or Tony Soprano.

"Me and the boys here we will each have a pint of Guinness and my beautiful wife will have a glass of Pinot Grigio... very cold." He pauses.

"Would you like food menus?" I asked ready to deliver.

"No need." He says abruptly. "What are your two favorite dishes, Dollface?"

I clench my teeth at the repeat offense.

"That would be the Cliffs of Mohar Irish nachos. It is kettle cooked chips, melted white cheddar, steak, scallions, and onion jam. I'd also recommend our Molly Malone fish and chips. It's classic, not greasy and both are big enough to share." I pray he is satisfied with that answer as I do not care to play the guessing game any longer.

"That sounds fantastic. You sold me. We will have one of those Mo-here things and two fish and chips. We like to share in this family." He gives me a wink and a nod and I run back to the bar as quickly as possible without being obvious about it.

The family finishes their food, orders a second then the third round of drinks all the while the father continued his charm offensive. But as I am waiting for their Beyond the Pale Bread Pudding to come up, the older of the two sons decides to approach me at the bar. He has a sweet face and floppy, dirty blonde hair.

"Sorry for the big guy. I know he can be a bit much sometimes." He takes a seat.

"No worries. I've dealt with a lot worse than that working here. It is actually sort of sweet, you can tell he loves his family." I give him a half smile while I continue to clean the well bottles.

"Oh, we are not family. The Don is our pimp, he takes us

out once a month for a hot meal." He is one hundred percent deadpan.

I stop in my tracks and look up at him. "Oh...um...I...I'm sorry... I didn't mean to assume." I am frozen in his stare for several excruciating seconds before he busts out laughing.

"You should have seen your face." He laughs. "Yes, that is my dad, mom, and little brother. They are helping me move into my new place. I'm starting Georgetown Law in the fall." He mentions in a non-boasting way.

"Congratulations!" I can't hide the fact that I am impressed by this handsome if not slightly dopey man in front of me.

Ding. Ding. The kitchen bell rings.

"That is your dessert." I turn to look back to the window where Ralph is sucking his teeth while again leaning over the pass.

"Well, I better get back then, if it reaches the table before I do I'll have no hope of getting any." He turns back for his table but then stops. "Hey...I'm going to walk them back to their hotel around the corner when we are done. Could I come back and talk to you? I mean if you're not too busy?" He looks around at the empty bar.

"Sure. That would be nice. Now get back there." I point to his table. "I'm going to get the dessert."

Danny did come back, sat on the corner stool and chatted with me until last call. He took me by surprise, everything about him. We started dating three days later.

I continue to stare at the man I met in the bar that night as he lies next to me. Now he is my loving, stable, affectionate boyfriend. Danny is the type of man that women dream about. He is the type of man you feel confident taking home to meet your parents.

Danny is a good man, but all I feel inside as I look at him is that...I have to get out of here.

I have to leave. I have to finally listen to that blinding poster and choose my future. This is not it. This beige fucking existence is not my future. I am suffocating in a sea of five-year plans, stability and keeping up with the Joneses. I need something different...I need someone different. I raise myself up slightly on my elbows to double check that Danny is still asleep. My heart is pounding with anticipation. I'm finally going to do it. I don't want to hurt him. I just want to slip out now and we can deal with all the messy stuff later.

"Dan...Danny, are you awake?" I whisper from atop my perch.

Nothing.

I slide my feet off the edge of the bed first. The blonde wooden floor is shockingly cold. I sit there a moment and look back to make sure the movement hasn't startled him. I'm just about to take off for my clothes when...

"Not so fast." Danny rumbles half asleep.

"I have to go." I squeak innocently, frozen over the edge of the bed.

"The sun is barely awake, you certainly don't need to be." He grabs me gently by the arm pulling me back down and into him. I curl under his arm as he holds me loosely. He smells of sleep and Irish Spring soap. For a moment, I am enveloped and intoxicated by his safety. It would be so easy to stay here, but then I see an image of myself at forty still dreaming about the man I always loved and never had the guts to tell.

Jumping back up I tell him, "I have to go. I have things to do today."

Danny places his hand on my arm again, "I'll make you pancakes." He is gentler this time but isn't giving up.

"I'm off carbs." I shoot a glance back at him lying on the bed.

"Then eggs, any way you want them. Scrambled, sunny side up, poached." He continues, his hand still on me.

"Poached? Gross. No." And with that, I am up and off the bed.

My jeans are up and struggling over my chubby thighs when he hits me with... "You're doing it again."

"I'm doing what again?" I really hate those open-ended statements that I'm clearly supposed to know the ending to.

"Whenever we get a little bit too close you pull away. You go cold."

Ouch.

I can hear the frustration in his voice. Part of me feels bad because I know he is right about me, but I have to be true to myself. I pause for a moment contemplating what to say. I don't want to fight, so I continue to slide on my Rush tee shirt and flip-flops.

"Nessa, stop. Just give me a second here. God, I am messing this all up." I hear him moving on the bed, but I can't bring myself to turn around and look at him.

The moving stops, "Nessa, I think we should get married. Do you want to get married?"

Married? Immediately turning to him I see Danny kneeling on the edge of the bed holding a ring. A large, shining diamond on a gold band is glittering out of a red velvet box. It is dumbfounding to see. It almost doesn't look real, but I know he is a man who would spare no expense. His round eyes are wide open and watery. I can feel his emotions running through my own body. My insides begin to shake.

"You, me, a dog, some kids...it could be nice, right?" He begins to fidget at my silence.

I don't know how to do this. People dream of this moment their whole lives. They rehearse their responses and they practice their shocked smiles. Here I am scavenging my brain for any remote thread of human feeling. I am desperately trying to find the words to end this nightmare. I'm so much better when I can prepare my words, write them down and send them off.

Slowly I start to put my thoughts in order, "Danny...we are not getting married."

He smirks. "Give me one good reason why we shouldn't."

Silence again. I wasn't expecting him to challenge me at all.

"Well?" He pushes.

I sit back down on the bed next to him.

"I guess I could stay a little while longer". I barely have it out of my mouth before Danny has ended my ability to speak. His mouth is on mine as he slides the ring onto my finger. I can feel the tears roll down his cheeks as he kisses me. All I wanted was to get out of answering the question. All I want is to get out of here, but now I've sunken deeper in. *What have I done?*

Before I know it, I am laying back in bed, under the covers and curled under Danny's arm as he strokes my hair. He knows that is my kryptonite. I'm immobilized the moment anyone plays with my hair. I start floating somewhere between a dream and a song. My hand rests on his chest. It gently raises and lowers with each breath he takes and his heartbeat tickles my fingertips. Would this really be such a bad life? Danny is kind and stable. He clearly loves me and he could certainly provide me with a comfortable life. There is something important to be said about that. He is the only man that I have ever been with where I could say that. The most that the other men I've dated ever had going for them was that they could provide free Tequila at whatever bar their band was gigging at that night. Well...that and some of the most imaginative sex I've ever had. But, carrying amps and having your sheets smell of stale beer gets old after a while.

I don't know how long I have been lost in thought about the men and mistakes that came before Danny. I hadn't noticed Danny's hand fall away from my hair until a light snore growls in my ear. He has fallen back asleep. I close my eyes and give in to the warmth coming from his body.

"Nessa! Hey!" Georges striking face is in front of me.

George! Shit! My eyes open wide. I couldn't have been asleep more than thirty damn seconds this time!

This has to be something more, right? More than just subconscious synapses firing at whim? More than just brain juice being shaken not stirred? More than that one time I dropped acid in college coming back to haunt me? I knew dating someone in a Phish cover band was a total mistake even then. No, this has to be a sign. I don't see any other way around it. My mom always says we come from gypsies. Maybe this is my gift finally manifesting itself. Perhaps the powers dilute over the generations. It's not nearly as cool as hexing people, but if it can lead me to George I'll take it. If it can lead me to love then that is good enough for me.

Ever so slowly, gently I slide free from Danny's arm and out of bed. He doesn't notice. I can't just disappear, I have to end it once and for all or it will never be real. I'll end up right back here the same as before. I open my bag to grab the notebook and pen I always carry with me. The words flow from me effortlessly.

Dear Danny- You are the most delicious vanilla ice cream that money can buy, the kind with the tiny black flakes of pure vanilla whipped inside of it. But I need ice cream with chunks in it. I need candy pieces, swirls of sauce and a surprise in its center. I'm sorry. I'm leaving. It's over. With Love- Nessa

I don't dare breathe as I slip the note onto my pillow with the ring. Backing away, bag in hand I take in his face one last time. He is sleeping so soundly, no idea what awaits him when he wakes up. Sadness and fear catch in my throat for a moment but quickly fade away.

I make it outside and I'm free. I feel so light I start speed walking up the hill towards the metro stop and text Sami. I really hope she is home.

CHAPTER 2
THE CIRCUS

We didn't have much, our families. We weren't wealthy. No one drove fancy cars and our houses shared walls. In fact, you wouldn't want a fancy car on our narrow one-way street that allowed parallel parking on both sides. One-sixteenth of a mile made of blacktop that crumbled under your feet, pressed up against uneven sidewalk squares that carried children's initials and handprints. Green trees gave pleasing pops of color all the way down the street. Our little half of a city block was the old country. Generations upon generations of families lived in these houses. No one ever left, much like the mythical village of Brigadoon. My grandparents, my mother's parents lived across the street and two doors down. My grandfather grew up in that house and will tell you how this was once farmland with fields and chickens all around. My father's mother lived next door in a small in-law apartment that resembled a bird's house. My Uncle Tommy, Aunt Ginny, and three cousins Sami, Cat, and Iris were directly across the street. I couldn't have grown up in a better place, surrounded by family, filled with love and grateful for everything that we had.

Our other neighbors who made up the old country were not related by blood but were family nonetheless. Across the street next to my uncle were the O' Malley family, a big Irish family rivaling our own. However, they were much more on the dysfunctional side of the line than ours has ever been. Their matriarch tried her hardest to out decorate my mom for each holiday. One year we swore she stayed up until midnight on Halloween to make sure her pilgrim window clings made it into her front windows before ours did.

"We'll let her have it, sweetheart." My mom smiled suspiciously at me, "Christmas is coming."

This didn't mean my mother was feeling the charitable spirit of Christmas. No, it meant she knew that no one could out-decorate the Reilly's when it came to Christmas and it was a fool's errand to even try.

Just next to the O' Malley's on the right, there lived the Gannon girls. Three elderly widowed sisters who lived together. They were sweet with a smile and a butterscotch candy for anyone who came within ten feet of them. I swear they've been seventy years old since I was born, but to this day, can be seen puttering around their garden. To the left of the O' Malley's, the Kowalski family was snug in between my grandparents and my uncle. I grew up with their grandson Stan. He was named after Tennessee Williams' famous character, but in reality, was lacking the same brute charm and work ethic. In fact, he grew up to be inexcusably dull.

The Moletti family lived on our side of the street, just one house past my grandmother. They owned the Italian market around the corner and Mrs. Moletti made the best cannoli anyone ever tasted. They were a staple at every holiday, cookout and special occasion. Finally, of course, there was the Anthony family who lived directly to our right. Even though our section of the city was known as Little Athens, the Anthony's were the only Greek family on our street. They possessed the biggest yard on the block, which isn't saying much, but meant everything. We were a big Irish-Polish-Italian-Greek family. Four cultures together forming one very unique corner of the world.

The weather today, among other things, has me thinking of home. It is so beautiful I almost want to walk the whole way to Sami's new apartment instead of going underground to the Metro. There was a break in the swampy heat that D.C. has seen all summer. It's warm, but not humid and there is this cool breeze blowing through. It reminds me of the late summer barbecues at home. Mrs. Anthony always hosted them in their backyard. As I step onto the escalator and descend underneath the city streets I am transported back to the summer before my junior year of high school. I was sixteen years old and incredibly cool in my own mind. I thought I knew everything. Then again, I think it was Jane Austen who said, "It is a truth universally acknowledged that all sixteen year old's are idiots..."

Waking up this Saturday morning in mid-August feels like waking up on Christmas. We have been planning this day for a few weeks and it is finally here. The summer is almost over and the past two weeks since writing camp ended has been completely boring. I've read three books, six magazines and have logged two entries in my writing journal each day. I'm not even out of bed and I can smell my mom's famous Hawaiian cake baking in the oven. Pineapple, coconut, and vanilla all whipped up together have our little corner of eastern Pennsylvania smelling like Oahu. Jumping out of bed I head straight for my closet. I quickly throw on my jean skirt and pink Sex Pistols tee shirt. Then with a quick swirl of face powder, a swipe of eyeshadow and a triple coat of mascara I am barreling down the stairs to the kitchen. I barely feel the steps beneath my feet I am going so fast.

"Morning, baby!" My mom looks up at me with a gleam in

her eye from her position at the sink. "Good morning, smells delicious mom."

Sunlight is pouring in through the large bay window at the center of the kitchen. There is no need for electricity on days like today. Manufactured light would be an insult to the power of the sun. The floor feels warm beneath my bare feet and radiates upward to my cheeks. I am filled with pure joy because the day feels full of promise.

"Coffee?" I asked, rummaging through the cabinet for my favorite Tinkerbell mug.

"Mama called, she has been waiting for us to come over for coffee." My mom says as she pulls her famous cake from the oven. The steam, full of flavor floats up to my nostrils. I can't wait for the picnic! Mom sets the cake to cool as I close and lock the front door. We are off through the house, out the back door and on our way to the Anthony's house.

There are moments in our lives that seem to have no outward significance. They are small in the big scheme of things, barely worth repeating to another person. Yet, internally, deep within our hearts they are worth everything. They are significant beyond measure solely to us. This day was sure to be one of those moments, I can feel it.

Skipping across the small green lawn, I follow my mom's footsteps all the way to the gate separating our home from the Anthony's. Peering in through the screen door I see Mama Anthony is already elbow deep in the ground lamb that will later be transformed into her signature dish.

"Ela, come in, come in" she shouts orders to us through the storm door in her own Greek-English hybrid language.

Entering ever so gingerly, our bare feet tiptoe to the far side of the tiny kitchen. I take a seat at the table as my mom pours coffee into two unassuming burgundy mugs, as if in her own home. The smell in the kitchen is pungent. It is an oddly invigorating blend of coffee, garlic, mint, green peppers and oregano. As Mama Anthony cooks away, we talk about everything under the sun from our families and neighbors to current affairs and politics. We don't always agree, in fact, we nearly ever agree, but that doesn't ever cause any change in our love for each other.

"Eat, eat." Mama points to me and then to the plate of Kourabiethes. I break open the sweet, date filled cookie and give one half to my mom to dip in her coffee.

Nearly an hour and a half in the kitchen and still no sighting of George. I obviously can't ask about him because that would be so painfully obvious I would die. My mom would give me her patented sideways glance, knowing that my casual conversation was not so casual. I fiendishly grab another cookie from the plate, but this time I do not offer to share. In fact, I am so un-casual I feel as if all the hormones in my body are boiling up in what could only be described as a witch's cauldron inside of me. I try to push it down with large bites of date filling, but I feel as though I will simply bubble up and explode when I hear the front door crack open. But it is the laughter that cuts through our kitchen conversation that instantly calms the cauldron. In fact, it feels as though all of the liquid in my body has drained out and left me empty. Unmistakable. Loud, but not obnoxious. Boisterous, but not overwhelming. It generates joy and creates more laughter no matter how far away you are when you hear it. At the front of the house, we can hear George and his dad, Papa Anthony carrying on and laughing as they come through the front door.

"What, they are donkeys now?" Mama Anthony mocks the men's laughter which gets my mom and I giggling along with her.

"Ay, ay, ay who's a donkey?" Papa Anthony strides confidently into the kitchen. He puts his large hands ever so gently on mama's shoulders looking over at what she is making on the stove.

"Oh, ho ho, picnic time, picnic time." he sings. "Hee haw, hee haw." Mama pokes fun at him before kissing his cheek. Without missing a beat, Papa looks to my mom and me before reaching for the coffee pot. "You need a refill?" I open my mouth to answer, but I am cut off...

"Nessa!"

My heart stops. George is standing in the doorway to the kitchen so coolly holding arms full of grocery bags. I have no idea how long he has been standing there. I was so enthralled watching Mama and Papa playing. He looks different from when I saw him last. He is no longer clean shaven, he has a very meticulously groomed goatee now. He is also dressed much more mature in a fitted black t-shirt and dark washed jeans. There is something different about him, he seems much more grown up than he ever did to me before. It hits me over the head just how out of my league he really is.

"Marshmallows!" He smiles tossing the bag across the kitchen at me.

"Chocolate bars, graham crackers and extra skewers in the bag. I will not throw those. That would be dangerous." There is mischief in his eyes.

Slightly confused and still reeling from seeing him for the first time in months my mouth won't catch up to my brain. I sit there dumbstruck and staring up at George for what feels like a lifetime, but could only really be a few short seconds.

"Oh, I forgot." Mama starts dramatically, "Nessa, will you make us the s'mores?"

"Of course," I respond. I introduced Mama to s'mores last summer and ever since it has become my specialty of sorts. I chalk it up to the fact, that I put an obscene amount of chocolate on each graham cracker.

George's eyes widen, "No wonder she is looking at me,

like who is this guy throwing marshmallows at me! Nessa, I apologize. How are you?" He asks with genuine curiosity.

Taking a moment, I scrounge up all the confidence I have inside me and I look up straight into his eyes, "Good. Great. Super!" He is still smiling at me. "Super!" He repeats with a wink.

Oh god, I can't bear to hold the eye contact any longer. I stare into my nearly empty coffee mug. Ugh, I am so lame. *Super?* I sound like such a dumb girl. I never want to be a girl like that. I want to be smart and edgy and sort of intimidating too. I imagine George likes women that are like that who are witty and intelligent too. While I'm drowning in my own self-deprecation it seems George has seamlessly disappeared upstairs and I am left slightly red in the face, sipping my coffee and replaying his entrance over again in my mind.

"Well baby girl, are you ready to go finish up the cake?" my mom says with a knowing push. She knows I am bound to be caught up in my own thoughts for a while and will need a reprieve. "Yes, we should do that," I respond weakly. She always seems to know how I am feeling as I am feeling it, sometimes even before.

Three hours after leaving Mama's kitchen and the picnic is in full swing. The sun is directly overhead, giving everyone in attendance a slight glisten of sweat. Thankfully the Moletti's brought over their yard umbrellas to provide some relief from the late summer heat. I have found a shady spot against the house that offers the best people watching perspective. Plus, it has the added bonus of saving my nearly translucent skin from burning. The Kowalski's are playing Bean Bag Toss in the alley just outside the yard. My mom and mama are running around putting out all the food and plates then more food and more plates. And the trio of my dad, Papa Anthony and George are expertly manning the grill, each with a beer in hand.

For a sweet few minutes, I get to watch and write completely undisturbed. It is as if I can't even be seen. I never go too far without my notebook. My latest one has a modern art style cover, triangles of bright colors and the O' Shaughnessy quote, "We are the music makers and we are the dreamers of dreams." I want so badly to be a writer, a real writer of novels or maybe even movies. I just want to be able to say something important, something that will make a difference to someone somewhere. So, I just keep writing and writing and hope something good comes out of it eventually. Maybe one day they'll make movies of what I've written. I could be famous. My family could be rich. We'll all move out to a big house in California.

"What are you writing?" George says, pulling me out of my daydream. I was so engrossed with my writing and dreams of grandeur that I hadn't even noticed he'd left the grill, circled round to where I was sitting and now was standing directly over my shoulder.

"Everything," I answer, squinting into the sky to look at him. His smile is so beautifully broad it beams like a second sun in the sky.

"That seems like an awful lot for one little notebook. Can I share some shade with you?" Before I can answer, he is pulling up a lawn chair next to mine and we are both sitting with our backs against the wall watching our family, friends, and neighbors.

"So, everything, huh?" George says as he attempts to peak into my notebook, but I pull it back before he can see anything inside.

"I write what I see, what I know...or think I know rather. I write about life."

I hope that sounds smart.

"So, you want to be a writer I take it?" George asks with a smartass manner.

I lean in as if to tell him a secret, "More than anything. I love it. I want to travel the world and write about everything I see and experience. I want to tell stories."

"Am I a part of your stories?" He asks keeping with the secret sharing tone.

Uh, um. Shit.

"No," I say quite unconvincingly.

"No?" George questions sounding somewhat disappointed.

"No, I mean yes, but no not really. You're in it...but not like in it. You know?"

There that'll convince him.

"I am part of the menagerie before us as it were." George's voice sparkles.

"Yes, exactly!" I jump. "I mean look at everyone. Different lives, different languages all moving in different directions, but it all comes together and inexplicably they somehow make sense to each other. It's a perfect mess."

George takes a moment to absorb the view in front of us and then turning and leaning into me... "It is the circus, you see. The clowns, the acrobats and the lion tamers alike in the three rings. They are all here and we, Ms. Reilly, we were born into it."

George's words suddenly transform the world before my eyes. In the first ring, my mom and Mama Anthony are wearing clown noses and oversized shoes. They are working their double act arranging and rearranging the food. In the center ring, my dad is in a preposterously shiny tuxedo with a whip before the untamed grill. In the far left third ring, the neighbors are clad in all too revealing leotards as they perform their death-defying polka on a tightrope that runs the length of the yard. Imagining it all makes me smile, but also leaves me with a terrible feeling of dread inside.

"Do I ever escape, run away from the circus?" I look to him for hope.

"I believe the phrase is run away with the circus." George retorts.

"But, I don't want to be a clown or a lion tamer. I want so much more than the circus has to offer. There has to be more out there, right? I mean you know. You left." I can't seem to hide the indignity in my voice.

George's playful air immediately becomes more sensitive. "I left, yes...but I always come back. I'm back right now under the big top with you, am I not? You see the circus, with all of its beautiful freaks will always be here for you. It will be ready to welcome you back. So, when you do go off to write about the world, you will always have a place, a family, a home to come back to."

"I suppose it is nice to visit the circus once and a while." I think aloud to myself.

"You will always find the people who love you under the big top." George catches my eye and then looks away taking a sip of his beer.

"I guess you might be right." I open my notebook and slyly write exactly what George said word for word.

"I will leave you to it," George says as he stands.

"Thank you...for opening up my eyes to the circus," I say. He in turn just smiles and saunters over to the food table to grab a stuffed grape leaf.

He is so even, balanced and self-assured. He is the complete opposite of me. I am constantly at war with myself. My heart and brain are frequently splitting off and traveling in different directions. I question everything and never feel satisfied with the answers. I am always left wanting more.

I close my eyes, shutting out everything and everyone in front of me. The sun moves behind a cloud and I enjoy a cool breeze as it blows through my hair.

CHAPTER 3
TALK FAIRYTALE TO ME

I open my eyes and I'm back above ground in D.C. I'm in a part of town that I've only ever been to once before. It was that one time in freshman year when my roommates and I thought meeting Marines at a nightclub we'd never heard of was a great idea. Newsflash...it was not a great idea. But this is where Sami lives now, probably the only section of D.C. where gentrification hasn't completely changed the land-scape. It is a sea of muted color apartment buildings without so much as a box store or coffee shop in sight. Sami has always been the daring one in our relationship. Where I wouldn't want to live more than a few blocks from my favorite caffeine, she doesn't blink an eye.

Sami, my sweet, but tough older cousin and I were lucky enough to grow up like sisters. Seeing as I am an only child, I credit her for keeping me from being a spoiled mess. Sami is always pushing me out of my comfort zone and challenging me to see what isn't easily observed, but this new living arrangement even seems a step too far for her. The directions in her text message read to go around to the alley behind the building to find her door. Brown door, number 1357, it reads.

As I turn the corner, I see the alley is scattered with slumped over bodies. I lose my breath as adrenaline pumps through my lungs instead of oxygen. It is good to know my fight or flight response is working. I reach into my bag for some protection. My shaky hands are clumsy and out flies an ugly white envelope onto the ground. I bend over quickly and return it to the bottom of my bag. My one-hundredth 'thank you, but no thank you' letter to top off the collection. I grab my mace and grip it tightly as I take my first step forward. I continue walking towards the door, realizing that the bodies are neither dead nor going to attack me. They are not sleeping, but barely awake. I can see a set of eyes looking up at me from the huddled mass on my right. Heroin tends to take away that get up and go quality in a person. Why is she living here? I see her door is only a few steps away now. Seconds go by like minutes getting to her door, but to my surprise none of the people I see in the alley even move a muscle or seem bothered by my presence at all. It's obviously comforting, but completely unnerving at the same time. I press the buzzer and a shining voice cuts through the dead silence of the alley like a siren.

"Come on up sweetie!" Sami sings through the speaker and the door unlocks.

That was rather nonchalant of her. The interior of the building looks like it might have been nice at one time, fancy even, but utter neglect has left it without hope. There is dust an inch thick on plastic orchids next to the door. What may have at one time been a cheerful peach color on the walls is now a muddy shade of brown. The short walk down the hall to apartment 102 is musty and the thick air turns my stomach slightly. Before I can knock on the door, it dramatically swings open and Sami pulls me into the apartment and into a hug all in one fell swoop. It is like traveling through the wardrobe and into Narnia. The apartment is fresh and clean sporting eggshell walls with a lilac trim. It smells of cinnamon rolls and Paul McCartney's Dance Tonight is playing in the background. There are no large lighting fixtures, but rather small lamps perfectly placed around the room mixed with large white Christmas bulbs. The space feels warm and looks quirky. It is quintessentially Sami. But, I can be happy for her in a minute...first...

"How did you know it was me and not a serial killer at the door?" I scolded

Without blinking Sami responds, "Even the serial killers don't like this neighborhood."

"Yeah, I noticed your neighbors in the alley are a lively bunch" I probe.

"Must be payday" she doesn't skip a beat taking my hand and guiding me further into the apartment to turn on the coffee pot.

"Was living at your sister's place really that bad?" She can't sway me from my line of questioning that easily.

"I'll take a one-bedroom with junkies downstairs over three screaming infants any day." She shoots me with a piercing look.

Sami, her sister Cat and I all ended up in the D.C. area for college. Cat met her wife Sara while they attended the University of Maryland. They both went on to Law School at George Washington University and started extremely successful careers. They have the most gorgeous brownstone in Georgetown. Sami moved in with her sister Cat and her wife a little over a year ago to get back on her feet after her job was unceremoniously cut from the school budget. It was perfect. Sami found a new teaching position, was saving money and bonding with her older sister in a way they never had before. Well, it was perfect until the In vitro fertilization took hold and landed Cat pregnant with triplets.

Unable to argue that point any further, I concede, *truth*. I know I certainly wouldn't be able to hold it together any longer either.

"Plus the metro is literally a minute away, my commute to work is cut in half and I no longer have a car payment. Now, tell me how beautiful a job I've done in here." Sami demands.

"It is beautiful. A haven, really." I smile taking in the whole scene.

Suddenly, very serious Sami says, "Thank you. Now, tell me why I am packing my suitcase furiously? I mean who sends someone a text reading- pack a bag for any occasion, I'm coming over?"

Not quite sure how to paint the entire picture, I pour myself a cup of coffee first.

Knowing me better than anyone Sami comments, "Liquid courage I see."

I take a sip and dive in head first...

"I broke up with Danny."

Sami looks shocked but not necessarily surprised. "Really? Why? What did he do? He isn't some kind of secret freak is he?"

"Danny? Please!" I spit out my coffee at the thought.

"He is a bit soft isn't he?" Sami admits, picking her words carefully.

"Yea...he um, he... He asked me to marry him." I don't even look up at her as I say it.

"And?" Sami jumps.

"And what?" Looking up at her now.

"What did you say?" She is now leaning across the kitchen counter peering at me. I look back down at my coffee, unable to look her directly in the eye.

"No. Obviously," I say quietly, feigning sadness.

"How did he do it? How did he take it? Did he cry? He looks like a crier." She isn't giving up.

I turn around to refill my cup and buy myself some time. I

know I should have been straightforward with Danny, told him to his face that it was over. I just couldn't risk losing my nerve and staying with him forever.

"Nessa!" Sami has had enough of my evasion techniques.

"He asked me this morning. He was in bed on one knee and I was half dressed." I blurt suddenly. Then reining myself in, I continue, "I didn't say no. After he fell back asleep I left a note on the bed and snuck off while he was sleeping. I don't know if he cried. He probably cried." I turned to glance up to meet her eyes.

"A Dear John letter?" I can hear the disappointment in her voice. "What did it say?" Now I feel even worse, knowing what I am about to tell her.

"I called him vanilla ice cream. Told him I didn't want that kind of beige existence and that I was leaving in search of Oreo cookies and caramel sauce."

I feel like the lowest of the low, but in her truest fashion Sami steps silently around the counter to where I am standing and puts her arms around me.

"You always did have a way with words." She whispers and we both crack a smile.

"Sometimes, I wish I didn't," I admit while wrapping my arms around her and resting my head on hers.

Without moving a single inch, "Do you think he's read it yet?" Sami asks.

"Well I have six missed calls from his mother, what do you think?" I take a step back to show her my phone.

"Yikes! She is terrifying! And, so now you must flee the country, right? You think she has a hit out on you? Is that it?" Now pouring herself a cup of coffee, the mood in the apartment has relaxed with Sami's first sip.

"I hadn't really thought about it like that. Seems a bit farfetched even for that family...right?" Sami shrugs at my question, although we are both a bit shaken by the idea.

"I'm sure she is just mourning her unborn grandchildren. Danny is a sweet guy, he will find a girl who really loves him. I'm not that girl." I comfort myself with the thought.

"And, one who loves to cut the crusts off his sandwiches?" Sami asks, always quick on the draw.

"And finds his Saturday morning cartoon watching endearing," I laugh.

"And doesn't mind that he giggles during sex." Sami jabs.

"God that was distracting." I exhale.

"I mean I don't know how you ever got off." She follows up.

"Determination..." I suddenly feel quiet. "But really though, I didn't want to hurt him."

"Of course you didn't sweetie, but you don't seem all that upset about it either." Sami rubs my arm.

I finally sit down on the white wooden stool next to her, "That is the saddest part, I think. I'm not sad at all. We were together for nearly two years. It is the longest I've ever been in a relationship with anyone. You'd think I'd feel something. Wouldn't I?"

"If you don't feel something then it wasn't right. If it wasn't right, then you were right to leave. Bottom line." Sami barely finishes her poetic advice before jumping to her feet.

Obviously feeling the need to perk up the conversation, Sami takes my hands and leads the way into her bedroom. The shockingly short journey through the living room does take my mind off of Danny and on to the adventure at hand.

Her bedroom is lit with white Christmas icicle lights zig-zagging across the ceiling. The walls are the same lilac color as the trim in the living room with eggshell around the border. Pictures of smiling faces and prints of Degas are scattered around the room. Her bed is so high off the ground I wonder if she needs a step ladder to get into it each night. It is brilliantly adorned with a comforter that looks like stars in the galaxy. On top of the bed, is a small suitcase sitting wide open, but empty while a pile of clothes is built up right next to it.

"What is it then? Why the sudden need to flee the capital?" Sami asks as she picks up a pair of jeans and begins to roll them into the tiniest mound she can possibly create.

"I've been having those dreams again." I start folding clothes along with her.

"The George dreams?" Sami says with a mixture of concern and intrigue in her voice. "Oh no." She knows exactly what I am referring to.

"Oh yes," I confirm.

"Oh no. I thought they had stopped?" She stops folding.

Sami has seen the aftermath of too many George dreams. All throughout our college years, she woke up when I would in the middle of the night crying, screaming and laughing. She listened over breakfast as I agonized over each excruciating detail. Most importantly, she took me out and made me meet real flesh and blood men when I would simply refuse to believe anyone out there would mean anything more to me than a quick thrill in the bar parking lot. She's been with me through it all, it only makes sense that she be with me now.

I shake my head. "They did stop for a while. For a long time actually, I was fine. I barely even thought about him. It has just been the past few weeks they have started again. Every freaking night there he is. My eyes are barely closed for a minute and he appears. Then this morning, I woke up and I just...I just snapped. It all became completely clear to me. I have to find him."

"He did always have a very dream-worthy quality like Uncle Jesse meets Freddy Mercury. But after all these...wait."

Sami stops she is just staring at me. She isn't moving, she isn't sipping her coffee or folding her clothes. Her eyes are fixed on mine and there is absolute silence. I don't think there has ever been this much silence between us in our entire lives. Then...

"What do you mean find him?" Sami finally asks suspiciously.

"These dreams have been slightly different. In them, I am seeing him in different countries, different cities. They are incredibly specific. We are together and happy. I think that maybe they are trying to tell me something. Maybe they are telling me to go out and find him. And hey, you and I, we always talked about backpacking across Europe!"

I am really hoping that last little spin sells her.

"Backpack across Europe to look for George?" Now it seems she is even more suspicious. My plan may have backfired.

"Yes...and no. It will be our quarter-life crisis trip, our adventure, we will follow the dreams and if we happen to find George along the way...then it was meant to be, like fate." I give Sami an unwavering, confident look and a slow smile crawls across her face.

"I love it when you talk fairytale to me." She says before taking a sip of her coffee.

A rush of exhilaration flows through my body knowing now I have her on my side. Damn, I am good, no wonder I am the top seller at the restaurant.

Now back to folding, Sami has a bounce in her movements, "And your dreams, they will be our strange cosmic roadmap?"

"Yes," I reply, happily scrunching pairs of socks inside of her shoes.

"I mean what is a tax return good for anyway, right?" She giggles.

I've always been thankful for Sami's beautiful sense of logic. I start packing her leopard print wheelie bag with the tightly folded jeans and tops, squeezing each as close to each other as physically possible.

"Alright, then I think we should start in London. That is where he was in my dream was last night. He even said so, he mentioned it specifically. I think Virgin Airlines flies direct from Dulles, but I couldn't get great reception on the metro. After we pack can we look online, alright? Then we can swing by my place, so I can pack and we are off. I really hope there is a flight we can get on tonight! Shit! I have a shift tonight. I'm supposed to be behind the bar all weekend. I'll send out some texts to see if any of the girls want to pick it up. Otherwise...well otherwise I don't know. Maybe I'll just quit. I hate it anyway, and I won't have trouble finding another bartending gig in this town. This just feels bigger than that, ya know?"

I inhale sharply. I'm out of breath, I am so excited I feel like I am thinking and speaking a million miles a minute.

Sami's face has gone very still again in reaction to my monologue. She asks, "Can I just play devil's advocate here for a minute? Your families are so close, couldn't you just ask your mom to talk to his and find out exactly where he is so we can go straight there?"

"I wish it were that simple, but no way. I don't want my folks or his to know I'm looking for him. I don't think they would really understand why or approve. They would just meddle, it would create way too much drama. Plus it's all top secret, anyway."

"What is all top secret?" Sami's interest clearly peaked.

"His work..." I start.

"Yes, I never believed that traveling nurse story he would tell at picnics." Sami interrupts.

"Well, all his mom and thus my mom knows is that he is in Europe somewhere working on a project. That is where he has been for the past few years. All other details are on a need to know basis." I shrug.

"And no one needs to know," Sami says using her television mystery announcer voice. And then returning to herself, "That is pretty hot."

"Don't even get me started." I shake my head in agreement, "Plus, my dad was always a bit suspicious of him. I could never get a read on whether he approved of our friendship, let alone anything more romantic."

"Reasonable, since you totally loved him and he was a grown ass man, twelve years older than you!" Sami retorts throwing her lacy red bra across the bed at me.

"Whose side are you on?" I ask with the proper amount of pique.

"Yours, always, forever, go-on." Sami smiles.

"We just never even had a chance. We never had a moment. The timing was never right. By the time I was old enough that he might be remotely interested in me, he was gone. And now, it has been seven years since I've seen him and for the life of me, I just can't forget about him. I can't help thinking if we just saw each other again and I could tell him how I feel, maybe things would be different. Maybe he feels the same." The weight of my emotions pull me down and I plop onto the bed.

I can feel Sami crawling across the bed to the side where I have melted and she puts her arm around me. "Well then, what are we waiting for, huh?" She says with an encouraging nudge. We both slink back off the bed and I pull her in for a hug.

"Thank you," I say through a few stray tears.

With one more bra, a knit hat, a stick of deodorant and Sami's giant purse we are off and out the door.

The air outside has changed and it feels like my life is about to, as well.

CHAPTER 4
COSMIC ROADMAP

The sun is shining bright golden rays in the sky, but the air is beautifully crisp and light. It feels like fall in the northeast, like a trip I took to Connecticut in October, once to be exact. I'm reminded of warm apple cider, pumpkin patches, sweaters, and boots. This is my absolute favorite weather. It is the most natural anti-depressant there is. A warm orange glow illuminates the tree leaves above my head. All of the people smile as they pass me by, even their little dogs stop for a sniff and scratch. It feels as though I am living out a scene in a movie. I'm smiling so wide and so hard that I can feel my cheeks meet my ears. I am simply radiating joy. I can't stop, nor would I want to. This has to be the happiest, maybe even the best morning of my life so far, and I have a feeling that it is only going to get better as the day goes on.

"One very large, foamy, chocolate powdery cappuccino for the beautiful lady."

I look up to the source of the deep almost gravelly voice and my already wide smile grows. The voice in front of me is initially only a dark shadow of a man against the bright sun behind him, but as my eyes adjust they focus on the sharp curve of George's jaw. He is smiling down at me holding two beautifully large mugs.

"The Dutch sun suits you." He kisses my cheek as he places one of the almost comically full mugs down in front of me. This is easily the best part of this trip.

"I think this might be my favorite place in the world." I beam back at him.

He doesn't sit across the tiny round table from me, he pulls his chair right up next to me. He leans in, taking my hand in his and we watch the beautiful people of Amsterdam. Each one is like a model. They are tall, slender with white blonde hair and the perfect spattering of tan freckles. We are simply mesmerized by them. His arm against mine feels exactly right like we are melding into each other, becoming one. Early morning turns to midday which gives way into the delicious dusk of evening. Sipping, chatting, laughing, and kissing the day away. This is what being in love must feel like. I know now that I've never been in love before because nothing and no one ever felt like this. I look back at George's handsome face. His eyes envelop me, and then he starts shaking my hand. At first, it is gentle, playful, swinging it side to side. Then suddenly, he is shaking it violently back and forth. He is looking at me and shaking my hand so hard it is vibrating up my arm. I'm stuck in his eyes, unable to look away.

"Nessa! Wake up!" I hear his voice though I don't see his lips move once.

"Wakey, wakey, eggs and bakey." His voice is changed, unrecognizable.

And with that, his face is gone from my sight.

Everything goes black.

I gasp.

"Must wake up. Must fight jetlag." Sami's ivory skinned

face is inches from mine. Her, wild, curly blonde hair surrounding me like a mosquito net in sub-Saharan Africa.

My eyes adjust to the sight in front of me and I remember where we are...London. We did it, we actually made it to London. A place I have wanted to visit my entire life and now we were here. He had been here too...in my dream. The whole flight over I imagined us clutching each other on the London Eye as it climbed higher and higher into the sky. Kissing as it hit the apex of the circle. Sami blissfully slept the whole six-hour flight while I stayed up unable to sleep. I stared out the window, dreaming eyes open. Saying goodbye to everything in my past and looking forward to the dawn of my future. I couldn't even write. My notebook sat open on the tray table without a new word placed in it.

"I have our whole day planned." Sami breaks back into my consciousness by jumping onto the bed next to me. "Full English breakfast at the pub on the corner, underground to Abbey Road for pictures and general worship, back down below ground to the globe and then hit Parliament, Big Ben and Kensington Palace. I figure we can walk most of the last three. According to my map, anyway. And we'll just grab a bite to eat down around the Palace later in the day. Maybe at the original Hard Rock Café? I think that it's not too far from there. But either way, we have got to get up and get started if we are going to see everything."

Her energy is so sweet and childlike and right at this moment completely overwhelming. I so badly want to dive into her day. I want nothing more than to happily traipse across London with her until we drop from exhaustion, but the dream is haunting me. The sensation of George's arm on mine still lives on my skin. I scrunch down on the bed stretching out my arms, torso and feeling the blood course down through my body.

"Coffee?" I roll my head over to look at Sami next to me on the bed.

She is already fully dressed. Face full of makeup, hair perfectly messy, torn dark grey jeans, black ankle boots with studs around the perimeter, and her favorite all black t-shirt with John Lennon's face outlined in white. It is completely fitting as she has always been the Lennon to my McCartney. Sami is the girl who walks into a room and everyone in it immediately falls in love with her. Where most girls, myself included, would use that to their advantage half the time she doesn't even realize it. That is the biggest part of her charm.

"There is nothing in this place that remotely resembles coffee, so that is why breakfast is the first stop on the hit parade. Now, up...up." She smacks me playfully on the legs before she herself jumps off the bed and over to the window. "This city is just electric, isn't it? I can't wait to get out there and really explore." She looks back to gauge my reaction.

"Sorry. I know we didn't see that much yesterday." I apologize while pulling my jean skirt up over my hips.

"No, please don't apologize. Spending the day at the Eye was a very...relaxing first day here. We were near the water and all the people watching. It was great. Really. You thought George was going to be there, so we had to go obviously." Sami's sincerity warms my heart.

I slap on my black tank top, rose-colored shawl and brown boots before whipping on some makeup. I don't want to waste a moment of the day, but I still haven't quite figured out how to tell Sami that I want to jump on the next flight to Amsterdam either.

On the walk from the hostel to the pub, I am absolutely silent. Still reliving the dream in my mind, I know I am making Sami uncomfortable because she hasn't stopped talking since we closed our room door. There is nothing that tweaks her out more than silence. And to me, there is nothing more unnerving than not having the words significant enough to break the silence.

"Do you think there will be a lot of people at Abbey Road? I'd really love a picture of just myself walking across the street without anyone else around. And of course, I want one of the two of us crossing together. So hopefully some people are around, just not too many. Gosh doesn't the air here just smell different in London? Like they pipe Earl Grey into the streets with one giant air freshener. Or little air fresheners on every corner. That would probably make the most sense. The pub is called Kit's, you know like Christopher Marlowe. He was known as Kit. Of course, you know, duh. But that is why I picked it. Here we are." Sami stops with a hop at the entrance.

Kit's pub has an unassuming and faded navy blue awning with gold letters over a large bay window. Walking inside we are hit in the face with the most delicious smelling food. I'm absolutely starving and can't wait to dig into the eggs with beans and toast. Sami's face is absolutely glowing with joy. We have both been complete anglophiles since childhood. The interior of Kit's is dark cherry wood from floor to ceiling with brass fixtures. There is a long bar on the left-hand side and three small alcoves to the right. Sami and I seat ourselves at the tiny two top by the slightly frosted window where we can look out at the people as they pass. I still haven't said a word. Luckily, the very young waitress quickly interrupts our awkward tension.

"What'll ye have, loves?" She simply charms.

"Cappuccino," I say softly, noticing the quiet in the place.

"Same...and a Strongbow, thanks." Sami orders confidently. "We're on vacation!" She responds to the shock painted across my face at her order.

"No, no judgment. I'm impressed." I smile, calming her.

We both sit silently, our heads propped up by our hands as

we watch the businessmen and women walk quickly by to the underground station next door. Above Sami's head hangs a production photo of the Royal Shakespeare Company's production of Dr. Faustus. It looks like it's from the nineteen sixties.

"Alright, cappuccinos each and a cider here." Our very sweet server surprises us both with the quick service.

"Thank you." I offer.

"Cheers," Says Sami, picking up the local vernacular.

"Anything to eat then?" Our waitress, who uncannily resembles Pippi Longstocking aims the questions at Sami. She is clearly the more approachable of the two of us right now.

"Full English please, for both of us." Sami can barely contain her joy.

"One to split, like?" She asks suspiciously.

"One each," I confirm.

"Ah, that's my girls." She says before taking off with a twirl to behind the bar.

"I like her," Sami says before taking a sip of her cider. "Makes me want to just take off, move here and work in a pub."

"Trust me, pouring shots and serving greasy food isn't all it's cracked up to be," I say over the edge of my coffee cup.

"Of course. I know that. But it would be different doing it here, wouldn't it?" She picks up her cappuccino, alternating her drinks expertly.

I look around the pub and it's quiet even though there are people in each nook and cranny. There are no loud televisions, just music playing softly in the background. There is another server behind the bar. He is a baby-faced giant of a man ever so delicately steaming milk and pouring it creatively over shots of espresso. It does look completely foreign from any bar I've worked at in the states and I've seen my fair share.

"Yea, I think it would be different actually. Maybe one day we will do it. The two of us owning our own little pub. You never know, right?" I look into Sami's eyes, she looks happy and slightly relieved.

Sami takes another sip of her cappuccino followed by her cider, "You had a dream last night, didn't you?" She takes aim right for me and my melancholic disposition this morning.

"I did," I say straightforwardly, not ready to divulge the details quite yet.

Her eyes are watching me very closely. "He wasn't here in London, was he?" She clearly knows the answer but doesn't want to actually hear me say it.

"No." I look out the window.

"Here we are, loves." Two heaping plates of food are placed before us. "Anythin else you'll be needin?" The ginger-haired server asks with a toothy smile.

"No, thank you." Sami looks up at her before starting in on the fried eggs.

After a few bites in silence Sami pauses, "So where are we going to?"

I look up from my beans and toast to see her looking quiet sympathetically at me.

"He was in Amsterdam, we were in Amsterdam together. It was...Sami, it was blissful." I can't help but smile at the make-believe memory.

"And you want to fly out today don't you?" Sami's voice is lower than I think I have ever heard it before.

I take a bite of the extra wide, ham-like bacon from my plate. The chewiness buys me time on the conversation. I hate disappointing Sami and I absolutely know that I am doing just that.

"We can still go to Abbey Road after breakfast. We can

still do all of the photos and do all of the worship. If they have a gift shop, we will totally splurge in the gift shop." I try to sound bright and sunshiny about the whole scenario.

"I don't think there is a gift shop. It's just a road." Sami responds through a barely opened mouth.

"I'm sorry." I put down my fork.

"Don't be." She responds before taking a double sip of cider.

"Are we okay?" I asked grabbing her hand as it rests next to the almost empty pint glass.

"Of course!" She smiles weakly, taking my hand in return. "This is the plan. You dream and we go. We are going to find him wherever he is. Where was he, again?"

"Amsterdam." I'm trying to hold in my unbridled joy.

"Amsterdam! How incredible is Amsterdam? How amazing will it be when you find him surrounded by daffodils, waterways, Van Gogh paintings and space cakes! That definitely says love my friend." Sami is genuinely glowing within the picture she has just painted.

"It does, doesn't it? I really feel like this is it, this time. I feel it even more than I felt it about London. Amsterdam is the place." I finish off my cappuccino in one fell swoop.

Sami takes another double sip of cappuccino and cider. "Amsterdam is the definitely the place. I can feel it too."

We finish up our meals and say our goodbyes to the sweet ginger waitress who now feels like an old friend. As we exit out from the deliciously cozy Kit's pub and into the overcast London day there is a peace between Sami and me. A peace that was noticeably missing just an hour ago as we entered. The day is gray and cloudy. It is exactly how you would imagine a London day to be.

"I'm just in love with its gloom." Sami looks up to the sky wistfully.

She always does come alive during the dark months.

When most find themselves suffering seasonal affective disorder, Sami really shines. Not even two steps out into the street and Sami grabs my hand. She leads the way holding my hand tight in hers as we make our way to the tube station. I am immediately overwhelmed with love for my cousin. I mean I love her every day, but there certain moments where that love just bubbles all the way up to the surface like pouring champagne too quickly into a flute.

The last morning Sami held my hand like this we were seniors in college and the sky was just as gray as it is today.

"Sami!" I whine. "I only fell asleep three hours ago. Why is it so damn important that we go to breakfast this morning?"

But Sami doesn't say a word she just keeps trotting up the hill that leads from our apartment to campus. She holds my hand tightly ensuring I don't lose pace or even worse, curl up in a pile of leaves along the tree-lined path. I am more than slightly annoyed by her mission this morning, but as I raise my eyes up from the pavement I notice that Sami is wearing the exact same outfit we picked out for her date last night.

"Sami..." I start, but before I can say another word, Sami cuts me off.

"I haven't been to bed yet. I'm starving and it's The Grapes of Wrath in our apartment right now." She says completely monotone and completely unlike her.

I don't think she is any more ready for me to push the issue than I am to be busting my ass up this hill, so I hold off on my questions. We are nearly at the top of the hill anyway; the dining hall is teasingly close. Stopped by the traffic light I take a moment to examine Sami. All the while she stares out into the street, not even moving her eyes as the cars fly past us. She is wearing the same outfit as last night, but it looks wrinkled and pulled at. I guess that makes sense if she has been wearing it for fourteen hours. Her makeup is blotchy, but not like mine is, from simply falling asleep without washing my face. Hers is perfect in some spots, but her eyes are basically washed away as if she has been crying.

The light turns red and again Sami is pulling me through the streets of Washington D.C.

"I can't believe of all the places you want to eat it is at the dining hall," I say with bewildered amusement as a cornucopia of smells hits my nostrils. And believe me, they are not all pleasant aromas. "We could have driven somewhere decent."

Sami shoots me a look as she hands the bleary-eyed cashier her card for us both. "You are still too drunk and I am too angry to drive. Also, this is literally the only place I can get coffee, a waffle, French fries, and ice cream at the same time."

She has a valid point. But, why is she so angry?

Sami finally releases my hand and we go our separate ways for food. Always having a bit of a sweet tooth she heads straight for the waffle bar while I dig into bacon, eggs and make a plate of cheese fries for us to share. We meet up at our usual table, a two-seater just up the stairs to the loft off of the main dining room. It is absolutely dead in here at this hour. I let Sami get through about half of her waffle and coffee before I decide to ask.

"Sami...what happened last night?" I try to make eye contact with her, but she isn't looking up from her waffle. "Sami?" I push her to answer.

"I broke up with Ryan." She says through the frog in her throat.

"Did he do something to hurt you? Because I will twist that creep up so fast." I set down my coffee mug a little too hard and some of it sloshes over the edge.

"Nessa, relax." Sami finally looks me in the eye. "He didn't hurt me. He stood me up. I waited, sitting at the bar for nearly two hours before he texted me back telling me he forgot we had a date. That's the fourth time in five months. I mean we've been dating eight months, I shouldn't be such an afterthought at this point." The passion has returned to her voice and although, I can tell she is hurting I am thankful to see the real Sami in there. That monotone zombie version of Sami scared me.

"No, you shouldn't be an afterthought at all. The first thought, always. Did you two talk about it at all after the first couple of times?" I ask seeing as this is the first time Sami is revealing this to me.

"Excuses each time and each time I would forgive him, but I'd still feel bad inside. It made me feel more and more insecure. I don't want to be that girl, Nessa." Sami's voice fills up our private dining area.

"What girl?" I ask, genuinely curious as to where she is going with this.

"I don't want to be the sad girl or the mad girl. I don't want to be the girl sitting on the edge of the couch or a bar stool or anywhere just staring at her phone waiting for him to call. Each time I felt myself getting angrier by the minute, then sad that he had forgotten me and then angry about being sad. No, I won't be the girl who is made a fool of. I don't want to be disappointed and let down. I'm dependable. I just want someone I can depend on." Sami doesn't finish her last sentence without crying. I know she hates crying in front of anyone, so I immediately dive back into dunking greasy potato strings into ketchup until she pulls herself together.

After a few minutes, just before I am about to take a giant bite of bagel Sami shyly says, "Thank you."

I reach out and grab her hand as it clutches her coffee. "You deserve someone you can depend on. You are the strongest, smartest, and kindest woman I know. You don't

49

need anyone. Period. But if you want someone...they should be just as strong and smart and kind as you are."

Sami purses her lips together into a smile and finishes off her coffee. "On the bright side, I was offered the full-time spot at my school, so I'm officially staying in D.C. after graduation."

"Oh my god!" I yell through the bagel in my mouth. "Congratulations! I am so happy for you." I beam.

"Thank you! I am thrilled and relieved. I love it so much there. The faculty, the kids, working right near the National Zoo and Adams Morgan. It is a dream come true. And if you end up staying too, we can stay living together." Sami smiles her authentic open-mouthed smile and I am filled with such love for this woman.

"Well, I guess now is as good a time as any to tell you." Sami's eyes widen as I start to speak. "I was offered the internship in New York. I'll be moving up there over the summer."

Sami takes a deep breath before spitting out, "I knew it, I knew it, I knew it! I knew they would offer it to you! You are going to be like the real-life Sex and the City."

"It's only six months to start and I don't know what I'll even be writing about yet." I can't allow myself to fully feel the excitement yet. It still doesn't seem real that I'll be moving in less than two months.

"Let's go out and celebrate tonight! Your big move and my big move. We are doing things lady and this town needs to know." Sami simply sings out her plan.

I peer through my rapidly closing eyelids at her, "Can we first sleep off last night before we plan tonight, please?"

"Deal." Sami chugs down the rest of her coffee and stands up. "Let's go home. This place is depressing."

It is absolutely freezing out. My fingers are numb, my toes are numb, and my heels are so cold they feel like shards of glass digging into my skin. I had no idea Paris could be so cold. I am wearing every piece of clothing I had in my suitcase, but the wind is cutting straight through each layer. My eyes are watering so violently that I can barely see the monumental Eiffel Tower as it looms over me. And yet, none of that matters, not even a little bit. Nothing could ruin my mood. I am here in the most romantic city in the world with the love of my life. I flex my frozen fingers through his and pull his hand closer into mine. The subtle sensation slows his pace as we make our way under the base of the tower. There is an inexplicable warmth emanating from his hand around mine. We are surrounded by golden lights and buzzing tourists. George spins me swiftly in under his arm. Our bodies are locked together as he ever so gently pulls my scarf down from my face to reveal my lips.

"You should not be here." He whispers, his lips now almost touching mine.

"What?" I could not have heard him right.

Before I can even get the word out of my mouth, George's face begins contorting in a way I have never seen before.

"I said you should not be here!" He screams, still only a breath away from my face. There is a guttural and unnatural depth in his voice. I am stunned silent and it feels as if everything around us has gone still. Nothing is moving, no one is even breathing.

My jaw breaks lose, dropping, giving way to a deluge of tears as George takes off. He turns like a flash and is bulldozing through the crowd.

"George!" I call out his name, chasing after him. Tears are streaming down my face. I don't know what has happened.

"Stop, please! George!" I scream out with everything I have inside of me.

He stopped. He heard me!

"George," I say with a whimper.

I'm barely able to catch my breath. The cold air feels like knives piercing my throat. I wipe the tears from my eyes to see George has turned and is walking back towards me. He stops just a foot away, far enough that I can't reach out to touch him and he growls...

"You really thought that *I* would be here with *you*? I would never be here with you! Never you! I am leaving you, Nessa. I am leaving you." And with that, he is gone, back into the crowd. Hidden by the night.

I fall to my knees feeling like I've been kicked in the chest. The lights swirl into a blur around me. I can hear the people surround me laughing, talking, and asking me if I am alright, but the noise of their voices sounds more like the tune of a carousel spinning out of control. I can't breathe. My lungs feel like they are shutting down, as they refuse to take in air. I try to expand them. I try to breathe deep, but the harder I try the smaller they shrink and I am starting to panic...Everything goes black.

"So, where was he this time?" I hear Sami's voice cut through the blackness.

I can't see her, but I can feel her lying next to me in bed. I'm sitting up straight as a board, drenched in sweat. My breath is quickly returning to me as I recognize my surroundings. I'm safe sharing this tiny bed with Sami. All of the ugliness was just a dream. I feel Sami's hand softly land on the top of my knee. Even under the best circumstances, she knows it takes me a few minutes to come out of my dreams and this has been unlike any other I've had before.

"Paris. We were in Paris." I take Sami's hand, unable to lay back down and relax.

"Should I boot up Ryan Air?" Sami asks without flinching. In fact, looking down at her she hasn't even opened up her eyes. I don't think she fully understands what this was. How different this felt.

"We were fighting. He was yelling at me. He was so angry. I was crying and screaming after him. What do you think that means? We never fight in my dreams. We've never fought in real life. He was saying he was going to leave me...Sami? What do you think that means?"

"I don't know. Damn it is burning up in here. Did you turn the fan off?" Sami drops my hand and is up out of the bed beating on the small oscillating fan in the corner.

"No. It must have broken while we were asleep." I squeak. Sami seems unusually irritated.

She gives the fan's buttons a few more pushes before sighing and moving on to the window. Motionless, I watch her from the bed. She lifts open the tiny window and sticking her head out into the city gives the saddest groan.

"Ugh. No relief. Did we really have to come to Rome in July?" She pulls herself back into the room to face me.

"He was here..." I start.

"In my dream." Sami matches the end of my sentence word for word.

Pulling her head back in and turning back into the room she rests against the open window. The moon is shining through strands of her blonde hair and she looks as if she should be starring in a foreign language film about an artist's muse. I reach down the side of the bed grasping for my water bottle but find the half bottle of wine Sami and I were working on before bed instead. I pull the bottle up to my mouth. The insanely cheap, one euro wine is dark and smells pungent. I take a swig from the bottle and my checks flush immediately. Sami has returned from her Fellini-esque reverie in time to catch me wiping the wine dripping from the side of my mouth.

"Well?" I extend out my arm to hand her the wine and without skipping a beat she accepts it.

"This won't cool us off." Sami swishes the wine around in the bottle for a few seconds before taking a swig.

"No. The dream." I press her.

"I don't know. Maybe." She takes an excruciatingly long sip from the now nearly empty bottle.

"Maybe, what?" I keep pushing forward. Sami is being unusually evasive and I am not exactly in the mood to go mining for answers right now.

"Maybe it means we need to stop chasing George across the damn globe. Maybe we should go somewhere that we really want to see and actually stay longer than twenty-four hours." Sami stops abruptly and finishes the bottle.

That wasn't evasive at all.

"What's the problem here? Haven't you enjoyed Rome? Or Amsterdam? I thought you fell in love with London. We wanted to backpack and that is what we are doing. We have seen so many cities already. Are you homesick?" I'm trying my best to understand where she is coming from.

I try to read Sami's eyes from across the room. She is still sitting in the window, but now I am fully awake, sitting cross-legged on the bed facing her.

"I guess I am just getting a little tired of the agenda." She says somewhat sheepishly.

"It has only been a little over a week! I am sorry you are feeling that way, but I have been in love with George since I was six years old. If I have the chance to actually find him now, I have to keep trying. I am so close I can feel it. I have to keep following these dreams. I thought you supported me." I plead with her.

"I do support you, of course, I do. But I want to go to Berlin, not Paris. Parisians are so...French." Sami walks away from the window and is now pacing slowly in front of the bed. I tilt my body so I can stay square with her.

"We can go to Germany after Paris." I offer.

"Until the next dream takes place in Croatia or Bulgaria. Sami's pace is quickening.

"What are you saying, Sami?" I stand to meet her.

"I'm saying you are being a little selfish. This was supposed to be our trip, our quarter-life crisis trip. I thought you said fate would bring George to us, right? Then let's let fate do its thing." She says with a matter of fact tone in her voice.

"We said we would follow the dreams. That was the plan." My frustration has reached my voice and it stops Sami in her tracks.

"Yes, we did, but I didn't think that was all we would do!" We are each now standing on our respective sides of the bed, but it feels like we are on different sides of the world.

"You can go to Berlin if you want. I am going to fly to Paris tomorrow morning whether you are with me or not. I will just come to meet you there afterward...no big deal, right?" I make eye contact with Sami for a moment before she pulls away. She doesn't say anything, so I take my laptop off the nightstand. The glow is blinding in the dark room.

"Seriously?" Sami asks and I look up silent. "Fine." She curtly ends the conversation.

As she climbs back into bed and turns her back to me I sit on the floor. The dark wooden planks are a cool relief from the heat of the night and the conversation. The glow of the screen changes color with each new page along with the booking process turning the tears on my cheeks into the saddest tiny rainbows. This is not what we had planned. I close the computer and listen to the sounds of Rome.

It is surprisingly quiet at night for such a lively city, but there is the occasional hum of a passing moped soloing against a chorus of mewing cats. The room is pitch black except for the warm glow of the moon bleeding in, ever so slightly from the window. I'm not ready to crawl back into bed so I pull my knees into my chest and lean back gently onto its frame so Sami doesn't feel me. Staring into the darkness, I hold my thick, pale legs close to keep myself from crying anymore. My fingers run over my bare skin, but stop and return to a smooth, raised spot on the top of my left knee. It is a one-inch scar shaped like a waning Crescent moon. It is actually remarkably close to how the moon looks tonight and the night when it first appeared on my skin. I trace its shape over and over again, until I can no longer feel where my finger ends and the scar begins.

"Sshhhhh-shit, why is it so dark out?" Sami unsuccessfully whispers as we peer out the screen door onto the normally well-lit street that separates our houses. Turning back to look into the living room I notice that nothing is on, no time appears on the television box and the green power light on Uncle Tommy's stereo system has gone out.

"Uh Sami, I think it's a blackout," I say as the room

begins to shift. Turning slowly and carefully back to the door Sami starts uncontrollably giggling at me.

"Bah...lack...out." She says over exaggerating every conso- nant, quite pleased with herself. Her voice sounds like a duck on helium and I start laughing so hard that my side cramps up. In fits of giggles, we end up in a lump on the floor. Thank goodness her parents are out for the night. I try to breathe deep between spurts of laughter to calm the stabbing pains. We pull our tequila and sugar infused bodies together long enough to stand back up at the door.

"Can you make it?" Sami stops me with a sudden, stark seriousness.

"I just have to make it across the street." I focus in, to match her new mood.

"Just? Just? Nessa! You have to open this squeaky as hell screen door and run across the street without being seen by any of our nosey neighbors. Then you need to open your gate, sneak to the back of your yard, and use the planting bucket to hoist yourself onto the mini roof and sneak in through your bedroom window. And if you haven't noticed my dear sweet cousin, you are very drunk."

I don't think she blinked once during that whole speech.

"Wow! You have really thought this through." I know I certainly didn't.

"I have more experience sneaking in and out. That's why I told you to open the window before you left the house. Now, go! My folks will be home soon and I have to fill my dad's Patron bottle with flat tonic water." Sami kisses my cheek, opens the screen door and pushes me out into the night.

The eerie darkness from the blackout gives me an imme- diate rush of fear which helps get me across the street in no time. I open the metal gate into the yard with meticulous care so as not to make a peep. I look back at Sami and give a wave before she shuts her heavy red front door. Still no sign of anyone around to rat us out to our parents. Excellent. Nothing goes unnoticed on this street, so this feels really special. Alright, I stay tight against the house until I reach the bucket under the mini roof. I can hear every step I take so perfectly. Crick, crunch, crack. The stones, grass, and leaves under my flip flops create a beautiful symphony that could completely give me away. All it would take is our dog hearing me beneath my parent's bedroom window. He would set off a siren of barks. I have to get out of my head and just go. If I think any harder I will panic. Crick, crunch, crack, crick, crunch, crack. I grab the bucket, step up, reach and "fuuuuuck!"

Ouch. Fuck. Shit. Ah man that really, really sucked. The stupid bucket turned over on me. Oh god, now I'm dirty and bleeding. Sami will be so completely disappointed in me.

"Nessa..." I look up from the ground to see a shadowy George just a few steps away.

"Nessa, are you alright?" George is talking very slowly. Or maybe I am hearing him slowly.

"You startled me." I cough, my mouth suddenly dry as the desert.

"Sorry, I did not mean to. I saw you scurry through the yard and then fall."

"You saw that?" I cut him off.

"I did." He says apologetically. "Are you drunk, Miss Reilly?" His sly smile creeping across his face. He is just gorgeous, even crouching in the dirt during a midsummer blackout.

"Nessa? Are you with me?" I can hear him and see him, but my ability to form words has ceased.

Nothing, I can say nothing.

"Nessa, your knee is bleeding pretty badly." George places his hand on my shoulder and I look into his eyes pleading without saying any words at all.

"Alright, how about we get you cleaned up and sobered up

missy." And with that, I am five feet above the ground flying over the grass in George's arms. I feel too safe to be embarrassed at this moment. George carries me across the yard and into his mom's kitchen. It is lit with white tea candles and a camping lantern. Setting me down gently on the chair closest to the sink, George extends my cut leg up onto the adjacent chair. He pulls a small flashlight from his back pocket and pops it into his mouth. Then he begins rummaging through the cabinets with one hand and flips on the water with the other like an octopus. Within seconds, he hands me a plastic cup full of water.

"Drink." He says sternly.

Pulling the cup up to my mouth I take a sip and the water initially tastes awful, I want to spit it right up. But it is cold and refreshing, and the more I drink the thirstier I feel. By the time George turns around from his scavenger hunt through the cabinets, I've finished my cup. He smiles and refills it for me before he sits on the other side of my leg. I drink down half of my second cup, but my stomach feels full and I don't dare push it any further.

"Ay!" I yelp as George pours Hydrogen Peroxide over my open skin.

"Sorry," George says. "You have got a good little gash here. It will only burn for a minute I promise. Keep drinking"

I lift the cup up to my mouth again and just hold it there as I watch George carefully over the rim of the frosted blue plastic.

First, he leans in and blows on the cut which alleviates most of the burning. Then taking a dish towel that he ran under the faucet, George ever so gently wipes away the dirt and grass surrounding the cut. He is swift and light, barely even touching me. He is completely focused, he doesn't look up to see me watching him. Zeroing in on the cut, he smoothly places a wet paper towel over the slice to soak up

59

the bubbling hydrogen peroxide and blood. The angry skin is red but clean and the burning has now completely stopped. George finally looks up and meets my eye.

"Well, the good news is you will not need stitches." George smiles as he opens up a big square Band-Aid that takes up my entire knee.

"Do you have anything in that kit for humiliation?" I try to lighten the mood.

Sealing up the sides of the Band-Aid, George laughs. "You do not need to feel that way in front of me."

"I should be a little embarrassed," I admit.

"No way, watching your little sneak attack on the house was the funniest thing I have seen in a long time. Until you ate it on a plastic bucket that is." He is cracking up. "You were all mission impossible and then kaboosh! You were on your butt." George takes way too much pleasure recreating the scene with music and sound effects.

"Oh my god! You're going to wake your folks!" I whisper trying to hush him.

"They cannot hear a thing. I promise you. Finished with your water?" I quickly finish the rest of my cup as George makes his way across the kitchen.

"Thank you for taking care of me." I sheepishly say bringing my leg slowly down off of the chair where it was resting.

"Anytime," George says with such genuine warmth in his voice that I believe he means it. It isn't just something he is saying to be polite.

"Well, this won't be happening again anytime soon...Sami convinced me to sneak out tonight." I scoot down into my chair a little further, feeling more at ease.

Popping the flashlight back into his mouth George dives back into the kitchen cabinets. He pulls down two mugs and a ceramic jar. Looking back he drops the flashlight into his hand seamlessly and says, "It is instant, so it is going to be gross, but it will do the trick." He winks at me before returning to his work, lighting the pilot light under the tea kettle and scooping whopping tablespoons of black grounds into the twin mugs.

"So what was it then that did you in? Beer? Wine? Something stronger, perhaps?" George asks leaning against the countertop next to the stove.

"Tequila Slurpees," I say with a grimace, remembering the taste.

"Tequila Slurpees?" George retorts with a grimace matching my own.

"Sami has a crush on the guy who works at the Seven-Eleven across the bridge. We drove over to see him, but he wasn't working. So we got extra-large Slurpees, came home, raided her dad's liquor cabinet and prank called the guy instead. The last part was my idea. Tequila seemed like it would be easiest to replace and Sami said it gets you drunk faster...it definitely did."

Oh god, I must sound so silly.

"Sami certainly has a nose for these nefarious plans, does she not?" George laughs as he pours hot water into each mug and then stirs them furiously.

"That she does. She has gotten pretty good at it. Her sister Cat taught her everything she knew, but Sami has definitely perfected it." I take the warm mug from George's large hands. The coffee smells potent.

"And this was your first time drinking I take it?" George takes a seat now in the chair closest to mine.

"Yea, why?" I blush.

"Extra-large Slurpee, tequila, attempting to the climb the roof of your house. You really went for it. You do not try anything by half, do you?" George looks me straight in the eyes. The light from the lamp is creating golden circles inside his hazel eyes. We both break the glance by taking long sips.

"Ugh," George retches.

"Why are you drinking it, too?" I ask with amusement.

"I have no idea. Solidarity I guess. The trick is to drink it quick enough not to taste it, but not so quick that it comes back up." George says before taking another long sip.

"I think I'm up for the challenge." I take another swallow. "So, what was it like for you? The first time you drank, I mean did you get stupid drunk as well?" I lean my elbow on the table.

"Believe me, you have a long way to go before you know the pain of getting stupid drunk. You know my parents always raised my brothers and I with alcohol. It was no big deal. We had a little wine with dinner and Ouzo at Christmas. But, my buddies growing up here were not raised like I was. So when we were sixteen, just like you, my pal Jimmy got a case of Pabst Blue Ribbon from his older brother. The two of us and a kid named Spiggs went over to the graveyard behind Saint Bridget's. We drank every can in the case. Well, I ended up puking on seven different graves; the front stoop, my mom's Oriental rug, the bathroom sink, the tub, and my bed. So, trust me when I say you have no need to be embarrassed in front of me." George firmly set down his mug after finishing his coffee with the end of his story.

"What did your parent's do?" I wonder aloud.

"My dad had me up at the crack of dawn scrubbing every inch of the house until it shined. My mom pursed her lips and refused to look at me for two days. I still do not know which punishment was worse." George nudges my hand to finish my coffee.

I take one last long sip and with a start, the whole kitchen begins to buzz. The sound increases until...pop! The bright white light above the kitchen table is blinding after sitting in the dark for so long.

"Ah, geez!" I rub my eyes only to realize my mascara has now smudged around my eyes and onto my hands. Excellent, now I look like a sad raccoon.

"I got it!" George jumps up and turns the kitchen light back off. We are back in the glow of the camping lantern. However, now a few blinking neon green timers remind us it is so far into the middle of the night that it has become early morning. I can see George notice the time.

"We should really get you home Miss Reilly. How is the leg?" George asks standing over the table.

"I think I'll live." I look up at him with a weak smile before standing to meet him.

"That is very good news. Alright time to get you up that roof!" Seeming almost excited, George opens the kitchen door out onto the back porch that connects our yards.

I step out and the air is much chillier than it was when I left Sami's house. My whole body shivers from the change, but before I can wrap my arms around myself George gently takes my right hand in his to lead me across the yard to the back of my house. A normally short journey now feels like a single heartbeat.

"Mr. Bucket you are no longer needed here." George slides the offending bucket against the side of the house where it belongs.

"What are you doing with that?" Looking up at the mini roof beneath my bedroom window I dread getting back up on that bucket, but it certainly won't work from all the way over there.

"You do not need it. Come here, I will give you a boost. Put your right foot in my hands and climb with your left." George squats slightly with his arms out.

"No way, I'll hurt you!" I step back. I am not climbing up him.

"I will be fine, you will be fine. You do not have much time before your mom will be up. I have you, Nessa. Trust me." George puts his hands together into a basket and I put my right foot carefully inside.

"One, two, three!" A swift push and I am up on the roof, my heart pounding through my chest. I am clearly not made for a life of crime.

"Are you still alive?" I hear George jokingly call up to me.

"Yes...I think so." I slide around on my belly so my head hangs over the edge of the roof where George is standing. "Thank you, George."

"Sleep tight." He says before turning to walk back across the yard.

As I slip both legs through my window and I am safely in the house I call down "Don't let the bed bugs bite."

George turns back again and says, "Get that cockeyed smile to bed". I watch from the window as he glides back into his house before I crawled into bed fully clothed and falling straight to sleep.

CHAPTER 6
WUNDERBAR

B eep. Beep. Beep. Beep. Beep. Beep. Beep.
     "Sami, the alarm."
Beep. Beep. Beep. Beep. Beep. Beep. Beep.
"Sami, hit the alarm."
Beep. Beep. Beep. Beep. Beep. Beep. Beep.
"Sami! Please!"

I feebly prop myself up onto my right arm. My whole body aches from falling asleep on the hard floor. My eyes just barely reach above the top of the bed. I'm sure Sami is still pissed and is just sitting there stewing, waiting to watch me wake up in a huff. But as I blink over the sheets, I see Sami isn't in bed. Sitting all the way up I scan the room and she isn't here at all. Her things are all gone, she must have left while I was sleeping. She left without even saying goodbye. Pulling myself up onto the edge of the bed the pit in my stomach begins to grow. I am alone, she is alone and I am no closer to finding George then when I was at home in D.C.

Beep. Beep. Beep. Beep. Beep. Beep. Beep.

"Fuck!" I can't believe she just left.

Stupid alarm. I stretch over the bed and hit the snooze button. I have to get ready and get to the airport. If Sami is gone then there is nothing for me to do now but go to Paris. I'll give her some time to cool off and when I get to Paris I'll call her to apologize. I'm afraid I'm still too fired up to do it now. We can work it out. We have to work it out.

The bright colors, sounds and smells of Rome have all gone gray. In fact, the whole drive to the airport and even the airport itself feels like a haze of colorless images. Drab and dreary is completely inappropriate for a city built on such a salacious history. The pit in my stomach is continuing to grow with each passing minute. It reminds me that I am by myself. It reminds me that I have driven away my best friend, the one person who has always been there for me. My only solace is the hope that this is it, this is where I will finally find George and all of this will not have been in vain.

About an hour into the bumpy, cramped and sleepless flight to Paris, the pilot comes over the loudspeaker. In a mysteriously accented voice he says, "Ladies and Gentleman, this is your captain speaking. We are currently flying at eleven kilometers above Switzerland en route to Paris. We have received word from ground control that the fog over Paris is too thick to safely land our aircraft. But not to worry, we have been rerouted to the closest open airport that can accept us which will be Munich, Germany. Our estimated arrival will be thirteen hundred local time. We are very sorry for this inconvenience. We will be sure to take care of all of your connecting flight needs once on the ground. If you have any questions, our knowledgeable flight attendants will be through the cabin to assist you."

Munich? No, no, no, no, no! The tears are rolling down my face without a sound. My breath is caught in my throat. I close my eyes not wanting to draw attention to myself even though every cell in my body is screaming. A sharp bump of turbulence shakes my breath free and I realize just how thoroughly I have fucked everything up. I suppress the urge to panic. The people on either side of me turn into walls of flesh closing me in. I reach up for the air vent, opening it wide and turning my face directly into it. I have to get through this, there is no other choice. I just keep repeating that to myself.

After what feels like the longest sixty minutes known to man, I'm off the plane and clutching the tiny business card the stewardess handed me. She had the most saccharin smile as if her endless cheerfulness would make the situation any better. I would have been much more comforted if her lips were pursed and she said: "sorry babe, this blows."

The airport is aggressively lit with white fluorescent lights. It makes my already tired eyes feel even weaker. Just outside the baggage claim area, I found a row of double-sided chairs that thankfully no one else has spotted. The quiet is soothing after the non-stop chatter on the airplane and subsequent walk here. Airport security insisted we all exit the gate area to either baggage claim or departures to speak with the airline face to face. It has been nothing, but a cacophony since the announcement that we were being rerouted. Standing in a line of impatient people pushing, yelling and complaining sounds like a fate worse than death right now. So I set out to find some peace away from the crowd. Here I am in a five square foot, steel, and leather German oasis.

It takes upwards of ten minutes to go from dialing the extraordinarily long number to actually speaking with someone from customer service. "No...nein...Paris...yes, Paris. I need the earliest flight out."

There is dead silence.

"Hello? The stewardess gave me this number." When the voice returns I almost wish for the silence again. "How can you not have another flight in the next twenty-four hours? Nothing, no space at all?"

I can't believe this.

"Well, can you provide accommodations or compensation?"

The voice on the other end now turns quite terse.

"Of course not. Danke."

The one bad thing about cell phones is not being able to slam them at the end of a terrible conversation. I dial Sami's number, but it goes directly to her voicemail.

"Sami, I know you are pissed at me, but please, please call me back. I'm in Munich right now, the fucking fog in Paris rerouted us. I am so sorry. Just please call me."

I stare at the phone in my hands and the tears return. This time I can't keep them silent, the sorrow is flowing through my whole body. I do nothing to stop it until I feel someone sit behind me, the force of their body on the seat bounces me slightly. I try pulling myself together wiping my red face clean knowing now that I'm not alone anymore. The air entering my lungs is slow and staggered. I've calmed the tears, but my sniffles continue to give me away.

"Sind sie in ordnung?" The deep voice attached to the body behind me speaks low and slow. I can feel them turn over their shoulder towards me. Jesus, so much for my oasis. All I want is to be invisible.

This is embarrassing. In hopes of ending this interaction before it even begins, I retort, "No sprechen das Deutsch."

I lean forward sinking my head down toward my knees in order to further separate myself from the stranger behind me.

"Oh, sorry are you alright?" The voice is softer in English, but I still have no desire to talk to anybody, but Sami right now. So I don't even answer this time. I know it is rude, but really what do I owe this complete stranger?

"Ok." The voice on the other end is clearly put off by my

silence to their kindness. I feel him turn his body back, no longer leaning over his shoulder to speak to me.

I sit back up in my chair tilting my head left toward him. "Yes, I am fine. Thank you for asking...I'm just a little sick that is all, I'll be alright."

"Do you need help?" I feel him lean his head right nearly touching me, but I can't make out the shape of him. I don't understand why he is being so generous towards me. Can't he see I am in a hateful funk and wish to be left alone? I guess I'll have to find another spot to sulk.

"Not physically sick...homesick, friend sick, love sick...I'll be fine." I grab my bag and stand. Wobbly-kneed, I turn to thank him quickly and leave.

"Thank you..." Standing above the kind if not pesky stranger I feel as though I've been sucker punched. The millions of particles that make up my stomach are exploding into my extremities. I am looking at the profile of someone I have seen a hundred times. Someone I could never forget. Someone I have been dreaming of seeing. The cut of his jaw, his round nose, and thick dark brown hair are all the same as I remembered. Now though I see the speckle of age at his temples. My fingers lose feeling and I drop my bag. My mouth is so dry I can barely squeeze out my surprise, I whisper... "George!"

Clearly shocked by my knowing his name, the man I had thought to be a nosey stranger turns his face up from his phone to look at me. I don't think I have blinked once, so I'm sure I look a bit like a crazy person. He takes me in, not saying a word. I panic. Dear god, maybe I am actually crazy. Maybe I have lost all of my senses and the man I am seeing is merely a mirage. He might just be a fever dream of the man I've been chasing around the globe placed onto an unsuspecting traveler's body.

"Nessa?" He turns his entire body towards me. Still sitting, he looks up at me his eyes full of questions.

The waver in my voice nearly chokes me completely, but I am able to cry out a simple, "Hi".

"Nessa!" In one smooth motion that takes me completely by surprise and nearly off my feet, George is up drawing me into his chest. His embrace brings years of memories flooding back to me. I feel small in his long arms as they hold me close, his chin leans up against the top of my head. I feel my hair catch in his five o' clock shadow and I can't help, but giggle. All the sensation I had lost at the first sight of him has shot back into my body. In fact, my senses are overloaded. I feel every fiber of his shirt beneath my fingers. I smell the same recipe of cigarettes and spicy cologne on his neck. I don't want this moment to end, but George takes my arms into his hands and he leans me out in front of him.

"Nessa, you are all grown up." He says with some humorous indignation.

"Have been for a while now." I smile back at him.

His stare is penetrating as he still firmly holds on to my arms, "Of course. It has just been so long." He pulls me back in for a hug and all of my weight sinks into him, I am weightless. "Too long if you ask me," I say diving deeper into the moment.

"Agreed." he softly growls in my ear.

I'm a million miles away, in a place that couldn't be more foreign, but I feel so very much at home right now.

"Meine liebe!" An energetic soprano voice directly behind me pierces the moment. George and I break into two pieces at the sound. I look back at the intruder who is incredibly close to us. She is tall, towering over me in four-inch black patent leather heels. Slender with pale skin, raven hair and peach cheeks, she looks as if Snow White walked out of the pages of Vogue. But she is paying no attention to me, in fact, she is looking past me. Her eyes are fixed on George.

"Meine schatzi!" Stepping past me George embraces the statuesque creature inches away from my body. She kisses him passionately wrapping her manicured onyx fingernails around the back of his neck. My tongue feels thick in my mouth like I am about to suffocate.

Turning back to me, George smiles. "Greta, this is Nessa. Nessa is an old friend from home. Nessa, this is my wife Greta."

The words ring in my ears so loudly I look around to see if anyone else has heard what George has said. He...he can't be married. This isn't right. This must be some awful joke. I feel nauseous like I might actually pass out.

Greta is inspecting every inch of me as I stand there silent, still in shock from the news. I feel like an insect under her microscopic gaze.

"Nessa, what an unusual name." Her voice drips like honey out of her perfectly pouty mouth. "It is so nice to meet you." She takes my face in her hands. They are soft, but firm as she kisses my right cheek, then after she passes my lips uncomfortably close she placed a kiss on my left cheek. She is breathtakingly beautiful and to top it all off she smells of freshly cut roses. If I weren't so angry at her mere existence I think I would be attracted to her.

I am standing dumbly in front of them. George...and Greta, their arms around each other and their eyes on me. I finally bring myself to open my mouth and speak.

"Yes...wife...hi...wonderful...wunderbar!" Oh, Jesus, I am spazzing out. Greta is looking at George as if I have some sort of mental condition, but when I look at him his eyes are gleaming at me. I can tell he is straining not to laugh in my face at my awkward attempt at speaking German.

I look down at the ground, staring at my beat up chucks.

"Nessa, how long are you in Munich for?" George asks, but looking up to respond I can only gaze speechless at Greta. "Nessa?" He prods for my answer.

"Until tomorrow night, I think. I was on my way to Paris, but they are having the um, the uh, the fog. So we were grounded here. No flights out until then." I give a weak half smile.

"Perfect!" Greta exclaims out of nowhere.

"Excuse me?" I shoot back immediately. It seems a bit rude of her to be so happy at my misfortune.

"Come and stay with us." She slips her arm through mine. "We never have any of George's friends from home in town." She has edged up next to me and we are facing George like two teenagers in front of their father asking to have a slumber party.

"I...I can't...I wouldn't want to impose." I try to break free, but she stands firm.

"No, no. You will stay at our flat tonight. We insist." George's tone comforts my uneasy feeling, but I can't do this. I can't see him with her in their home. It is just too much.

"I really, I don't know. You and your wife." I look at Greta next to me. "I..."

"Please, Nessa you must. You cannot possibly stay here at the airport." Her arm releases mine, but not before taking my hand in hers. She reaches out to George with her free hand and we are now standing as three.

"Yes, you must." George's voice is knowing.

"I don't know what to say...thank you both very much." I can only hope the fear I am feeling doesn't show through in my face.

"Nonsense!" Greta squeezes my hand. "It is our pleasure. Come we will take good care of you." And with that Greta is leading me away from George, away from my oasis, away from the overwhelming happiness I felt only five minutes ago.

"George, her bags!" She calls back to him without a second thought or glance.

In all the ways I imagined finding George, in all the fantastical scenarios I created in my mind, this was never one of them.

CHAPTER 7
IF YOU SEEK SAMI

It is too goddamn early for Britney Spears to be blaring on the radio, but nevertheless there she is gurgling ...*If you seek Amy*... Ugh.

Her thinly veiled innuendo plays over and over and over again until I want to bash my head into the window of this car or open the door and fling myself onto the Autobahn. Whatever my fate from the high-speed collision with the pavement would have to be better than being stuck in this living hell for one more minute. I would cry if I weren't so unbelievably angry with Nessa. No, the fiery anger turned all the tears I had into steam. So now I'm just a human pressure cooker sitting in the back of this sketchy German taxi.

Staring out the window I can feel my jaw clenching so tight that my teeth hurt. I can't believe she didn't even wake up when I left. I wasn't exactly being all that quiet about it. Or maybe she was awake but didn't let on because she didn't have the nerve to talk to me. The mere thought makes me even more furious.

"Miss...Miss...Miss, this is it." My taxi driver very sweetly speaks broken English. My attempt at German must have been so terrible at the airport he decided this would be easier.

The hostel I booked frantically on the airport Wi-Fi is plain and unassuming from the taxi window. It is just a corner building painted in a pastel, Easter egg pink. A white block letter sign above the door is the only tell-tale sign of what is on the inside. I open the door, step out of the car and straight into a puddle of cold, gray and foul smelling water. Awesome. I guess this is just how this is going to be. I wanted to come to Berlin so bad. I had to put my foot down. I had to leave Nessa in a foreign country and now the universe is repaying me by making my time here absolutely fucking miserable. I'm half tempted to just have the driver turn around and take me back to the airport. I'll go to Paris, I'll meet her there and apologize. Before the sweet driver can pull my wheelie bag and backpack from the trunk, I pull out my phone to call Nessa.

No voicemail, no text, nothing appears on the screen. And it hits me, she isn't thinking of me. She isn't trying to find out where I am or if I am safe at all. You know what, screw it. I'm here on my own and I'm going to have the best, miserable fucking time there ever was in a post-communist Berlin. But first, I need a nap. Without Nessa tossing and turning next to me all night, I might actually rest peacefully for a few minutes. I give the driver a handful of euro coins in exchange for my bags and march confidently into the Pepto Bismol® themed hostel.

After what feels like mere minutes I'm awake again. Berlin looks totally different when the sun goes down. I stand in front of the tiny window in my room staring down at a nearly unrecognizable street. Neon lights gleam through the thin glass. People are out on the street singing, talking, grabbing food from the carts that have set up shop for the drinking crowd. Down the street on the left, there is a small red and black awning, it looks like a divey rock bar. I'm seeing a lot of black clothing, band t-shirts and leather going in and out. I think I know where I'll be spending the night tonight.

The short walk from the hostel to what appears to be the bar of my dreams is a symphony of light, sound, and smell. It is the kind of scene Hunter S. Thompson would write about. With my first step inside I hear Dio's Holy Diver playing and a smile of contentment creeps across my face. It is fairly busy, but not so much so that I can't find a seat for myself at the far end of the bar. It's perfect. I'm not exactly hunting tonight so sitting alone at the end suits me just fine. I just want a few drinks and some good music to drown out the grim reality of the day.

I take my seat at the end of the bar, lean in to make quick eye contact with the bartender, then relax back and wait. Looking around at the ratted and worn metal posters on the wall I can tell the place has been around for a while. It most certainly has some history. Some of the patrons look a bit tattered and worn as well like they might have been here since opening day.

"What'll it be?" The man behind the bar startles me from my assessment of my surroundings. His hands are spread wide across the bar. I can tell he's tall even though he is leaning in to hear my order. His dark, nearly black hair is cut stylishly with one side hanging down near his equally dark eyes.

"Tequila. Whatever ya got, as long as it's silver." We both take each other in for a moment before he turns his back to the bar to pour my drink.

I examine the faces around the bar. They seem natural, at home here. The majority of them are clearly regulars.

Breaking me from my reverie once again, the bartender slides the shot glass in front of me. It's filled to the brim. As I wrap my fingers around the cool glass he places a salt shaker and slice of lime on a napkin next to my hand.

"No need for the training wheels, thanks." I raise my eyebrows at him before shooting back the smooth, nutty-flavored liquor. He gives a chuckle and a smile before tossing the lime in a trash can behind the bar. Just as he is about to move back down the bar, I order, "Another one, please?"

He raises his equally expressive eyebrows at me and grabs the bottle from the back of the bar. He pours another shot into the glass right in front of me without ever breaking eye contact. There is something immensely appealing about him.

"Thanks." I nod before emptying the glass for the second time.

I immediately feel the alcohol relax my muscles, warm my ears and lift my spirits. Before I can ask for another pour the bartender is pulled away by a very large, bearded man at the other end of the bar hollering something that only vaguely resembles the German language.

A song or two turns into five or six. Guns N Roses, Iron Maiden, Rammstein, more Dio. A shot or two turns into three and four. As the night goes on the faces dance. Not literally of course. No, they are weaving in and out of the dark shadows, neon lights, red paint, and leather.

"I'm sorry but you look far too smart to be sitting in this place all alone." The increasingly handsome bartender says, standing in front of me again.

"That's very nice of you, but you don't need to cheer me up. That is the tequila's job." I motion to my empty shot glass.

"Another?" He asks, clearly surprised.

I squint slightly at his disbelief, "Yes, please." I continue kindly.

"Alright. Tequila it is." He pours the shot. "And a water for good measure." He smiles as he fills a pint glass up to the top with the water gun.

"You're too good." I shoot back the tequila swiftly and follow it with a slow, dainty sip from the water.

He laughs, "Danke." And begins to move back down the bar.

"You're not German, are you?" I call out to him.

He stops, turns back to look at me, "Am I not?"

"You're British, right?" I'm almost certain of it.

He takes two steps back and very sternly stands just to the right of me. "Nothing gets past you, does it?" He smiles relieving my worry.

"Where are you from?" I take another sip of water.

"Little place, no one's heard of. So I tell 'em all London. I'm much more interesting from London." He gives a devilish wink and I laugh.

"I understand that. I've been telling everyone that I'm from Canada rather than the United States. It has worked pretty well for me so far." I admit.

"Ah see, I knew you were a clever one." He pauses for a moment. "So who is he?" Now directly in front of me, he places his forearms down on the bar and I can fully see the sleeves of tattoos on each of his arms. They are incredibly sexy and distracting and I suddenly realize he has asked me a question.

"Who is who?" I don't understand his meaning.

"The guy?" He asks, and I am more lost. Men with good ink like his always make me lose my cool a little.

"I'm not here with anyone." I smile motioning to the empty stools next to me.

"Yea, I gathered that already. I mean you're a gorgeous girl drinking tequila alone. There's got to be some bloke to blame for it. Tosser, I'd bet." He smirks obviously waiting for me to confirm his suspicions.

"Oh no. No, there is no guy. It is a girl actually." I feel sad for the first time since entering the bar.

He straightens up from his hunched over position, slightly shocked by what appears to be a revelation. "Sorry, I hope I didn't…I didn't mean to assume, or offend or anything."

"You didn't at all." I calm his nerves. "It's not like that." I continue to confound him. He has a slightly dopey, but sweetly confused look on his face.

"I'm completely lost. Do you want to talk about it?" His eyebrows ask in harmony with his voice.

"Do you?" I counter.

"Well we are known as excellent listeners you know." He smiles widely.

"Is that the royal we?" I tilt my head to ask.

"I mean barmen or bartenders as you yanks refer to us. As a people, we are excellent listeners. He has spread his arms wide apart now so there is one on either side of me. I feel all of his attention on me as though there is no one else in the bar.

I respond the only way I can think how, "Ahhhh, the bah-mayn. A docile creature with impeccable poouuring, shayk-ing, and list-ning skills. They are rarely found outside they-er natural habitat."

The barman stares at me blankly for a moment. "I don't follow."

"I'm working on my Steve Irwin impression," I say with all seriousness.

"It was, well it was awful." He's too much of a sweet-hearted guy to lie, the barman begins to blush slightly.

"Yea, it needs some more work. My Axl Rose is much better." I assure him.

"Now, that I would like to see." He smiles that same flirta-tious smile.

I return it to him saying, "Maybe one day you'll be lucky enough."

"Here's to hoping." He places a second shot glass on the

bar next to mine and fills them both. "Cheers!" We clink the glasses carefully and throw back the booze quickly.

"It's my best friend, she is my cousin actually. We are basically sisters." I say hanging my head slightly.

He leans his forearms back on the bar, leaning in closer to me now. "Go on." He says so softly you wouldn't imagine I'd hear it in this place, but the rest of the bar is completely irrelevant to us now.

"We are traveling together. Were, we were traveling together until she got it in her head to go to Paris alone." I lift my eyes to see him and he is watching me intently.

"Why would she do that?" He asks without moving.

"Oh because George is there. George must be in Paris, she saw the solid irrefutable proof in her dream!" I'm suddenly quite animated, "George, George, fucking George."

Even though he moves slightly back from our intimate position due to my spasmodic answer, the barman is still looking at me as intently as he had been when he asks, "Who is-"

"George?" I cut him off.

"I'm afraid to say yes." He gives a nervous look.

"George is the love of her life who she hasn't seen or heard from in almost ten years. He is living here in Europe. Somewhere. And she thinks she is just going to magically find him. No plan, no information to go off of. Nothing."

"Sounds like she's lost the plot." His eyes wide at the preposterousness of the story.

I shake my head, "She is actually super smart, she's just... I don't know how to put it." I sigh.

"Hopeless romantic?" He asks.

"No, it's more like a pathological need to believe in fate. Like she already knows the end of her own movie." I offer.

"No one wants to know the end of a good movie before it comes." He says matter-of-factly.

"She does." I shake my head again wishing she was right here with me now.

"I was devastated when my mate let slip about Bruce Willis in the Sixth Sense. I mean who does that?" The barman goes on very seriously about movie etiquette before realizing I'm staring up at him blankly. "But I digress." He wraps up.

When he is focused back on me I continue, "I just hoped she'd come to her senses, get wasted and make out with an Italian guy in a public place like a normal twenty-six-year-old."

"Charming." He retorts slyly.

"Don't judge!" I hit him with my best withering stare.

"Never!" He lifts both his palms to me. "Now tell me, what if she does find George? Say her instincts are correct."

That's ridiculous, "It's not going to happen. I mean, what are the odds?"

"Yes, but what if she does?" He leans closer.

"I um, I don't know." I'm shocked into silence for a moment by the thought of it.

"Does she know?" He asks almost in a whisper.

"I shouldn't have let her go alone." I feel anxiety drift up from my stomach and flood my head.

"I am sure she is fine." He attempts to calm my rising angst.

"No, I should not have let her go!" I feel the tears form behind my eyes.

"Then go to her!" The barman says clearly shook by my energy.

"Now?" I jump off the stool.

Throwing his hands out to slow me, "Hold on! I'd recommend letting the Tequila wear off first, maybe get a good night's sleep. Then tomorrow hop on a train or a plane."

"But what about the rain in Spain?" I sing with a sway.

"Right, you miss are cut off." He reaches his hand over the bar to take mine and helps me back up onto the bar stool.

"I was just playing! One last one?" I plead sweetly.

"Last one, on the house." He pours the clear liquor into my empty shot glass, though not all the way up to the top as he had before.

"You are the devil" I chide.

He smiles, "Like Pacino in The Devil's Advocate?"

I narrow my eyes looking him up and down. "No, more like Jack Nicholson in The Witches of Eastwick."

"Even better." A blush crawls across his face. The fact that he gets my reference is a complete turn on.

"So, what brings you to Berlin?" I ask, curious to know more about the man behind the bar and get my mind back off Nessa.

"School. I'm studying here full-time." He seems intrigued by my questions about him.

So I continue, "What are you studying?"

"Literary research. I'm working on my Masters in twentieth-century German literature." He says modestly.

"Wow!" That is unexpected.

"And you, what do you do or study?" He flips the table on me.

"Kindergarten teacher. Master in A, B, Cs and one, two, threes." I joke.

"To be honest, you'd never find an American girl this far outside the club district. We don't sell Bahama Bay Breezes here." He reaches out and twists one of my curls in his fingers.

"Breezes mess my hair." I take my finger to his chin and move his head so he is looking directly at me rather than my hair.

"You are different." He said seriously.

"I'll take that as a compliment." Neither of us breaking our stances.

"You should."

With that, the lights in the bar flash on violently and we are broken apart by the shock.

My eyes constrict from the burning fluorescent light above me.

"We are closing up." He says apologetically.

I take a handful of Euros from my purse and lay the money down on the bar before stepping carefully down off the stool all the while feeling the barman's eyes upon me. I don't want the moment to just end like this.

"I hope you don't take this the wrong way." I start. "But will you walk with me back to my hostel? No funny business. I just. I could use the company." I try to gauge his reaction.

His lips purse into a genuine smile. "Yea, I'd be honored. No funny business."

"Where can I go to smoke?" I ask, knowing I have to leave the bar.

"Out front. I'll be done in ten minutes." He says.

"Thank you." I extend my hand out to shake his, He shakes my hand with a laugh and begins wiping down the bar with vigor.

There are only one or two other people still in the bar when I walk out the front door. On the street, half of the neon signs have gone out, but the food vendors a block down seem to be doing alright for themselves. There is a coolness in the air that wasn't there five hours ago when I first came into the bar. The chatter and laughter down the street are unintelligible but familiar. I pull out a cigarette from my bag. The jewels on my purse catch the light from the bar's sign. It came free with a bottle of perfume and has a bedazzled Norwegian flag on it, so I always use it on nights out as a conversation starter.

Just as quickly as I caught the gems sparkling, the light goes out. Leaning up against the red brick I light my cigarette. Through the glow of the flame, I see a man rounding the corner on my left, just a few feet away. Even in the darkness, I can make out the lines of his face, he looks like he was once quite handsome. A strong chin and pronounced cheekbones are highlighted with salt and pepper stubble. The hood of his jacket is pulled up over his forehead casting a shadow over his eyes. His walk is slow and steady as he approaches. In the few steps it takes for him to get close to me, I can feel the muscles in my stomach tighten and my breath quicken. I am extremely aware of how alone I am right now. For a second I consider going back into the bar but know it would just be an overreaction. I inhale quickly on my cigarette and blow out the smoke in hopes it will form a force field around me. I look up to watch him pass and find his eyes, now visible, locked on me and his path is angled exactly toward where I am standing. He is muttering something in German.

"No Deutch," I say trying to keep him at bay. He stops in front of me and mimes smoking and manages a heavily accented "please?"

I hesitantly, weakly smile and reach into my bag for another cigarette to give him. I'm thankful that is all he seems to care about. Before I can hand it to him before I can even realize what is happening my back is pushed hard into the crusty brick wall. He shoves me into it so hard that the top of my head smacks the bricks from the velocity. His hands are pressed against my breasts and squeezing them so hard there are tears streaming from my eyes.

"Stop!" I cry and he pushes even harder against me.

"Help!" I try pushing him away, but his size and weight against me are much more than I can lift.

He shoves his dirty right hand against my mouth, but I

continue to scream through his fingers. I try to fight back, to wiggle away but I can barely move. He is pressing me so hard against the wall that I'm losing my ability to breathe.

His knee violently pushes my thighs apart. My tears and screams turn into sobs.

"Oy!" A familiar voice breaks the terror. In an instant, the hooded man is off of me. The barman is clutching the attacker's shoulder and in one fell swoop punches him straight across the face. The crunching sound resonates. He hit him so hard the hooded man stumbles into the road and without looking back runs away down the street.

After recoiling from the hit, the barman gently places his hands on my shoulders, "Are you alright?"

I try to squeeze out an answer, but instead, I just start crying and fall into his chest.

Wrapping his arms around my shaking body, he hugs me softly. "Come on, let me take you somewhere safe." I can't even look up at him. I simply nod my head against his chest in agreement and he leads me away from the bar holding onto me the entire time.

CHAPTER 8
GUESS WHO'S COMING TO DINNER

Greta's soft hand did not let go of mine once, from the time she took it in the airport until we reached their flat. Even then, I believe it was only because I told her I desperately needed to use the bathroom. The twenty-minute taxi ride felt like an eternity as I bathed in the horrific irony of my life. My eyes felt glazed over as they flitted from the back of George's head in the front seat to Greta's perfectly winged eye-liner, to my hand entwined with the hand of the most beautiful woman I have ever seen up close, who just so happens to be George's wife. By the time we reached their flat, I felt so nauseated I thought I might throw up at the doorstep. I didn't even take a moment to look around their home, I politely asked to be excused to the bathroom and made a beeline.

Five minutes in the tiny cerulean room slowed my heart rate and calmed my stomach. Looking around the immaculate, jewel-toned space I feel more like I am in a Moroccan bazaar than a two bedroom flat in Bavaria. The ceilings are high, which is unusual for European apartments. This place has to be expensive. I feel like I am on House Hunters

International scrutinizing every detail. My surroundings couldn't feel more alien, but there is also something very soothing and familiar about it. I can't quite put my finger on it. I know I am taking far too long in here, but I can't help taking a sniff around. The scent, that's what it is. There must be an air freshener or something in here. I have to know what it is. There is a wooden cabinet above the toilet. The wood is naked and if not for the intricate carvings along the sides it would almost look handmade. On the lowest shelf sits two tea lights with a metal birdcage in between. I pick up each tea light to smell them, but neither is producing the teasing scent. The clay bird inside the cage has a serene, dream-like expression as it sits upon a nest of potpourri. It is hardly the expression I would have in the situation, but I'm amused by the inanimate little creature. As I lean in closer to inspect his features it hits me all at once. Cloves. The potpourri is cloves and dried orange peels. Closing my eyes, I inhale deeply taking the scent in fully.

I can barely open my eyes as I slowly open the back door out onto the porch. Not that it matters much. There are no clouds in the sky, so there is nothing to keep the sun from burning straight through my eyelids incinerating my exhausted corneas. Staying up until five in the morning the night before a picnic was not the smartest idea. I shut the screen door quietly behind me since I am not sure if I can handle everyone right now. I may just slink back into the cool, dark house for another hour... or three. It's barely eleven and half the neighborhood is in the backyard already. The polkas are playing, meat is roasting and my mother is holding court with Mama Anthony under her brand new, extravagantly large patio umbrella. Actually, the meat smells delicious. I could seriously devour some kabobs right now and French fries and strawberry pie.

*Oh shit! Shit, shit, shit...*I'm still stoned. Eric promised me it would wear off by now. What a stupid ass he is. I swiftly dip back into the house for my sunglasses and a glass of water. As I try to seamlessly exit the back door of our house for the second time, I notice George sitting on his front stoop. Seems odd that he wouldn't be out back with the rest of the menagerie. I creep along the side of the house towards the street to get a better look at what he's up to. I'm surprised to find he's sitting hunched over with his elbows on his knees smoking a cigarette. Maybe he is feeling as out of sorts as I am this fine Sunday morning. I sneak out the front gate and past the freshly trimmed rose bushes that line the fence to the Anthony's front stoop.

"You look as bad as I feel," I whisper in a raspy voice, feeling like even with all the noise of the backyard our mothers will still hear us. I must have done well sneaking out front because George jumps at the sound of my voice in front of him.

"Hi."

"Nessa, Jesus!" George looks up at me without his usual smile.

Maybe I shouldn't have come up here.

"Sorry, I'll leave you to it." I take a step back, my heart pounding with insecurity.

"No, I am sorry. You just caught me off guard is all. Have they sent you to find me?" George doesn't look up from his cigarette once as he speaks.

"I haven't been to the picnic yet. I only just woke up a minute ago." This makes George chuckle.

"Rough night for the graduate was it?" He tilts his eyes up to look at me, though his head still remains facing down. "Nice sunglasses." He laughs. The George I know is now popping through this unusually gruff exterior.

"Ha! It's more like a great night, rough morning for the graduate." I move in closer so that the edge of the house hides me from the eyes that might spot me from the backyard.

Bobbing his head up and down, "I can commiserate."

"Can I bum, a cigarette?" I ask cautiously.

George lifts his head and takes a long look at me before taking a small, black, rectangular package out of his front left pocket. It feels like his eyes are burrowing into me. He hands me the slender, but firm cigarette and I instinctually roll it between my thumb and pointer finger. Still not taking his eyes off me he extends out his hand holding a lighter. In one rapid motion of his thumb, almost like magic, a large flame pops up. I've only seen this done in the movies before, so dear god don't let me screw this up and embarrass myself. I place the filtered side gingerly between my lips, still holding it between my two fingers I feel my hand shake slightly. I lean the tip into the flame and suck the heated smoke into my mouth before quickly exhaling. George flips the cap back over the flame and quickly returns the lighter to his pocket. I must've done it right. George slides to the street side of the stoop and leans up against the rod iron railing. He motions for me to sit next to him. "Your folks will kill the both of us if they see you out here smoking with me."

We both sit quietly for a minute. I can hear the party in the back, but the street out front is quiet, almost tranquil. I hold the cigarette up to my mouth and hold it there, barely breathing it in. It doesn't taste like I expected, it reminds me of the spice market on Second Street and my nana's Christmas ham.

"What brand of cigarette is this?" I try to sound as casual as possible.

"They are cloves." George glances sideways at me. "I had no idea that you smoked."

"I don't actually." I can't help but be honest with him. "I just wanted to give it a try."

"And?" He asks.

I inhale slightly. "I think I'd rather smell it than smoke it really."

George winks, "That is probably for the best."

"I do like the way it feels between my fingers, though," I admit.

"Well, you hold on to it then," George leans his head back on the railing. "So, was it the Tequila Slurpees that did you in again Miss Reilly?"

"No, but thank you for remembering that lovely display of elegance." I feel my face begin to flush.

"I am only teasing you. Come on, now," George elbows my arm.

"Eric had a party last night and he made brownies. He promised me I'd sleep it off, but I'm fairly sure I haven't." I lean my head back onto the concrete wall fully facing George.

"Eric, your boyfriend Eric?" George questions.

"I just feel like everything is moving in sort of slow motion. It's not bad it's just not a nice feeling I guess...I don't know. I'm ready to feel like myself again." I take a puff from the nearly dead cigarette only to remember why I haven't actually been smoking it this whole time.

"How much did you eat?" George prods.

"I don't know, he gave me one like this." I hold my thumbs and index fingers into the shape of a square. "I mean I've smoked pot before," I whisper again. "But never eaten it, ya know? Have you?"

Shaking his head, "What a moron. He should never have given you a whole one to eat. You can't really tell how strong they are until it is too late. In the future always eat little by little. Try a quarter of that size next time you try it."

"Of course, you know all about it. That was a dumb question." I slump forward feeling a little too vulnerable to be so physically relaxed.

"I have just had a little bit more life to live than you have yet. Do not worry, you will catch up and catch on and probably know much more than me very soon." George takes a long drag from the clove and there is quiet between us again for a moment.

"So, why are you out here? Why are you hiding from the family?" I tilt my head slightly to catch his expression. His lips contorted in a way I've never seen before, half smile and half grimace.

"Caught me," George stops talking, but it is clear he wants to continue, so I hold still and wait.

"I just got word last night that I am being transferred out of the New York office. Next week I am moving to Seattle. I have yet to tell my folks. My mom, she is not going to take it well." He throws the butt of the cigarette out into the street where it smokes for a moment before dying out.

"You don't have a choice?" I squeak. I feel absolutely devastated by the news. I want to break out in tears, but I won't dare let him see.

"No. They do not really give you a choice with these things. They say go and you go." I've never heard George talk this much about his job. He's been working in New York for the last five or six years. It's very unclear and no one really talks about it. Especially him.

"Maybe telling them won't be as bad as you think." I offer some hope, but George's look expresses how full of shit we both know the sentiment is. "Do you want to go?" I asked not able to look at him for fear of giving myself away.

"Yes." For the first time this morning I see a genuine look of joy and relief on George's face. My stomach flips inside my body. I feel sick. Partly from the news, partly from the clove and somewhat from the fact that I'm starving.

"Let's go get some food." I pop up from the step and get a bit of a head rush. "It will be fun. You can worry about telling them later when they're well fed and have a few beers in them."

"Yes. That sounds like a great plan." George stands to wave me forward and he closely follows my lead to the backyard.

"Nessa, are you well?" The sing-song voice of Greta through the door snaps me back to reality. Face to face with a clay bird.

"Yes, thank you. I'll be out in just a minute." I splash some water on my face and quickly exit the bathroom into the rest of the perfectly decorated apartment.

Walking out I catch a glimpse of George in a side room to the right. He is on the phone in what seems to be a home office. He smiles as he continues to talk. I give a quick wave and move down the hall towards the kitchen. It is a soft gray color and is decorated with jewel-toned candles mixed with copper photo frames. I walk through what appears to be years of memories. George and Greta holding pints of Guinness, one showing them on the beach in their swimsuits, kissing sweetly, and lastly a photo of them underneath the Eiffel Tower. Each photo that I pass pinches my lungs a little harder until I can barely expand them. I missed it, I missed all of it. I am seeing the life I could have had, right in front of me. She is cooking me dinner ten feet away.

"Nessa, darling, George said you would like lamb is that correct?" Greta pops her head from the kitchen into the hallway where I am slowly asphyxiating.

"Uh, yes...whatever is...easy. Please don't make a fuss for me." I feel like I can't find any words when I speak to her.

Grabbing my hand again Greta says, "Come on, let us have some wine. George will be out soon. Work, work, work, you know."

Sitting me on a barstool at the kitchen island, Greta pours me a very large glass of white wine. She is playing soul music softly in the background. Sam Cooke's "A Change is Gonna Come". She is humming along, this beautiful woman. Her heels are off so she slides around the bare floor in stocking feet. She moves effortlessly. I watch silently while every movie, television show, book and song I've ever known starts haunting me. They are telling me to hate her. They are telling me she is the enemy. It's like I've been preprogrammed to destroy her, but every fiber in my being is fighting against it. I find myself liking her. She is lovely and has been nothing, but kind to me. She doesn't see me as her enemy. I am no threat to her.

"Drink, drink!" Greta demands and so I do.

After a few minutes of drinking, prodding questions about my personal life, and cooing over me, George miraculously joins us in the kitchen. Admittedly, I am charmed by Greta, but it doesn't mean I'm exactly comfortable being alone with her.

"Sorry, I had a conference call I couldn't reschedule. What did I miss?" He looks at us both.

"A bottle of Pinot Grigio." I retort without much thought.

"You are just in time darling." Greta interrupts. "The lamb is ready and the table is set. Let us eat."

Greta leads the way into a small dining area attached to the kitchen.

We are only a few bites into our meal when Greta wallops me with...

"Did you ever hear how George proposed?"

I shake my head no.

"It has actually been a few years since we've been in touch." George jumps in.

"You will love this story." She starts.

"I am sure I will." I take another sip of my third glass.

"George is such a romantic." Greta's face lights up.

"I never knew." I look at George.

"I am not, really." He says sheepishly.

"You are being too modest!" Greta's voice rises above his. "We went away on holiday to Sardinia. You know, Sardinia?"

My lips glued shut, I shake my head in acknowledgment that I have in fact heard of the Italian island.

She continues, "It was the most beautiful place I have ever seen in my life. We had the most incredible three days. Then on our last night there, he woke me up in the middle of the night. When I opened my eyes, he had covered the room with tiny white candles. The window was open so the salt air off the sea filled the room. George held my hand." Much to my horror, Greta reaches out and grabs my hand recreating the scene.

"And he told me, he could see himself with no one else, but me for the rest of his life. He slides this magnificent diamond on to my hand and kissed me. Of course, I said yes. Who could say no to this man?" Greta releases my hand and I smile at her. I had thought the worst was over, but that last bit really made my heart ache.

I can tell she is looking for me to respond, but I can't. I can't think of a single damn word to say about her story, so I blurt out, "Dinner is delicious."

"That it is! Well done, sweetheart!" George jumps in right behind me offering his glass up for a cheer. It is almost as if he can feel my skin crawling from discomfort. For a blissful moment, Greta is silent, before she lands the second hit of her one-two punch.

"So, Nessa you haven't told me yet, are you involved with anyone? A boyfriend back home?" Her lips are thin and spread across her face like the Grinch, as I look up at her from my plate, mouth full of lamb.

"Do not tell me you are still with that punk you dated in high school." George teases.

"Eric was not a punk!" My voice shoots up three octaves.

Then turning my attention back to Greta with a more serious tone, "And no, I am not with anyone right now. Single."

"It is too bad you are not staying in München longer. I think you and my brother would really hit it off." Greta's eyes are penetrating me trying to read my thoughts.

"Nessa would not be interested in Ansel, he is not her type," George says with unshakable confidence.

In harmony, Greta and I now share the same thought as we retort "How do you know?" The combination of our voices and heads turning towards him must have been too much for George. He throws his hands up in the air.

"Down ladies! I concede." Then popping up, he grabs another bottle of wine from the kitchen to refill our glasses.

"If I were spending more time here, I would have loved to meet him. Perhaps we would have hit it off." I say out of politeness before escaping into my fresh glass of wine. I just hope it satisfies her and ends the conversation. Can't we talk about something easier like politics or religion?

Just as George sits back at his place there is a loud knock at the door. George looks straight to Greta and quite knowingly asks, "Are you expecting someone?"

Greta's sharp closed mouth smile breaks out into its full-face version. Lighter than air she floats up from her seat and kisses George on the cheek "Don't kill me, I just could not resist." She spritely flitters off from the tiny dining room, through the kitchen to the apartment's door. I can hear her greet the newcomer. "Hello, darling! Come in, come in we are just finishing dinner with a glass of wine."

I look to George for some sort of hint of what is happening, but I get nothing from him before Greta is back in the dining room with a tall, striking man behind her.

"Hallo!" He says with an accent slightly thicker than Greta's. "George, nice to see you brother," The stranger reveals himself as he takes George's hand for a firm handshake.

George gives him an uncharacteristically terse, "Hi."

The gorgeous stranger makes his way around the table. He stops above me extending his hand, "And hello."

I reach out my hand to shake his, "Nessa" I say introducing myself. But instead of shaking my hand he kisses it.

"Nessa, it is my pleasure to meet such a lovely lady." His voice is like melted butter.

"Smooth talker," I smirk as he releases my hand and takes the seat next to me.

Greta is bursting at the seams watching the scene unfold from her spot in the doorway. "Nessa, this is my brother Ansel! He just happened to be in the area and stopped in for a drink. Isn't that wonderful?"

Wow!

Ansel is staggeringly tall. He must be at least six feet, two inches. He is impeccably dressed in charcoal dress pants, shiny black wing tips, and a long sleeve black buttondown shirt that looks so soft and tight it could be painted directly onto his skin. His eyes are crystal blue like his sister's, but his hair is dirty blonde. It is shaved on the sides and just long enough on top to be slicked back with gel. Ansel's smile is genuine with thick lips encasing perfectly straight, pearly teeth. He looks as if he has walked off the pages of German GQ and is now sitting inches away from me, watching me intently, as though I am keeping a secret from him.

"Ansel is a restauranteur. He owns the most critically acclaimed, traditional Bavarian restaurant in München." Greta moons.

I feel all three sets of eyes burning into me.

"I love German food," I say, now fully confirming I sound as dumb as I feel.

Ansel picks up the glass of wine Greta has poured for him. He swirls it, sniffs it and finally takes a modest sip.

"Nessa, it would be an honor to escort you this evening. I can show you the town as they say." Ansel offers confidently as if he has never been turned down in his life.

I nearly choke on my wine at the proposal, but before I can say a word George jumps in to answer for me.

"Nessa just got here. She is exhausted. I am sure she just wants to stay in."

With that Greta's eye shoot from me to George with gusto.

"She is a young woman, she doesn't want to stay in with an old married couple." Greta fires, her eyes burning into George. I try to open my mouth to speak, but Ansel cuts me off.

"I only have the best intentions." He directs to George first. Then turning to me, "One night in München, it would be a sin not to see something of our city."

"And our city is most beautiful at night." Greta sings, looking back to me.

"I'm just saying she might not be comfortable going off with a stranger in an unfamiliar city," George says in an intense whisper.

I take another sip of wine seeing as I won't be speaking anytime soon.

"Where is your sense of adventure?" Greta blasts George's whisper out of the water.

I finish the last sip in my glass.

"Hi. Hello. Do I get a say in any of this?" By the looks on the faces around me, I can tell that what I thought was an internal thought became an external one.

"Forgive me." Greta reaches across the table taking my hand once more. "Of course, your opinion is the only one that matters." She bats her long lashes sweetly at me and then slides her eyes menacingly to the side of her where George sits.

I can't believe I am about to say this, but I know I can't stay in this apartment for the rest of the night.

"I would love to see the city with you, Ansel. If you would just excuse me for a few minutes I am going to go freshen up."

I stand slowly. I can feel the wine all the way down in my knees.

"Take all the time you need." Ansel stands as I do, the way old-fashioned gentlemen do in the movies.

I leave the stifling dining room to collect my bag in the living room. But before I walk down the hall to the bathroom I stop to hear the exchange happening in my absence.

"I cannot believe you would spring this on her!" George says in his terribly ineffective whisper.

"She is happy about it! She has gone to change her clothes." Greta glows.

"She is being polite! She felt obligated." George is no longer even attempting to whisper.

"I thought she seemed genuine," Ansel says slowly. He seems completely un-phased by the couple's argument.

"It is simply rude that is all. It is rude to invite her to stay with us and then pawn her off on your brother." I hear George stand up from the table.

"I will treat her to the best, George. Have no fear." Again, Ansel with all the mellowness of a cartoon caterpillar.

"That is not the point!" I think Ansel's relaxed demeanor amps up George's ire over the situation even more.

"What is the point, George? It's not like she has been very conversational anyway." Greta pushes herself back into the argument.

I was being plenty conversational! She has no idea what is going on here. She doesn't understand what I am feeling right now. I couldn't even put it into words if I tried. I storm into the bathroom so as not to add my own voice to the battle in the dining room. I quickly pull off my ripped jeans and t-shirt. I slip on one of the little black dresses I brought along with some savage, wedge heels. I didn't want to go so far as to put on my silver party dress that pushes up my boobs. Although I probably should. I had been saving it for my first night with George, but that's all gone to shit now. After I exit the bathroom, I throw my bag next to the sofa bed where I will be staying later and stand for a moment just outside the dining room. A weird silence has fallen over the room. So, I decided to just go for it. I pop into the doorway.

"Ready Freddy!" I bounce, trying to break the ice.

"Who is Freddy?" Ansel asks with a confused look on his stupidly handsome face.

"It's just a silly American saying. Don't mind me. I'm ready to go when you are." I sway back and forth uncomfortably. I can feel George looking at me, but I don't dare actually look back to confirm it.

"I wouldn't dare keep you waiting." Ansel stands so elegantly and in one smooth stride crosses the room to where I am standing.

Maybe this will be a good night after all.

Ansel slides his large hand behind my lower back and ever so gently guides me towards the door. As he opens it for me, Greta calls out from behind us.

"Nessa! Here is my key darling, in case it gets late." She winks at me.

"Thanks." I look at her gleaming at me like a mother sending her daughter off to prom. Then I see George step out from the dining room behind her. His eyes are deep pools, but I can't think about that. I look straight into him and give a simple, unfeeling, "Bye" before turning out into the night.

Ansel closes the door behind us and flashes his high beam smile at me.

We are only a step out of the apartment when I hear George yell.

"Unbelievable!"

Ansel directs me to my right and we pass the living room windows. They are glowing with bright white light from the kitchen.

I look back for a moment at the apartment as I can hear George and Greta's voices, but cannot make out what they are saying.

"Don't mind them," Ansel says. I turn my head around to look at him. "They have a very fiery relationship. My sister takes after our mother. She was Italian so, you know."

"Right," I say as carelessly as I can muster.

"Do you like music?" He asks thoughtfully.

I shake my head, "Yes, very much."

"Good. I have the perfect spot for you." His hand returns to my lower back as we continue down the street.

CHAPTER 9
GEORGE IN WONDERLAND

Jesus Christ, how did this night spiral so brilliantly out of control? In fact, this whole day feels like the Looking Glass. Only in this acid trip fairytale, I am Alice. So, I pour another glass of wine in an effort to stop the spinning. I throw it back in one swallow. I cannot just let her leave, not like this with his presumptuous hands on her. I must say something. I step out of the dining room and into the kitchen, but she is already next to the door.

"Bye."

Nessa's voice is light as the air, even though her green eyes are bullets shot straight into my head.

She has a unique knack for saying everything by saying virtually nothing at all.

And then she is gone.

I try to suppress it. I try to hold it in as long as possible, but the wine and the overwhelming sense of dread I feel do not allow me to hold my tongue.

"Unbelievable!" Out comes the guttural bark that had been building inside me. I aim it right at the back of Greta's head, at her perfectly coiffed jet-black hair. She stands there unmoving, the Queen of Hearts, she is plotting her next move very carefully.

"What is the problem here, George?" She pivots slowly on her toes back to face me.

"What you just did was incredibly vulgar!" I spit out.

I cannot fathom the fact that I even have to point that out to her.

"Vulgar?" Her voice reaches a pitch only the birds would be accustomed to.

"Yes, vulgar. You invite my friend here to our home and then unceremoniously send her off with your brother. A friend, she is basically family, by the way, who I have not seen in many years. What must she be thinking of us?" I implore her.

"You are overreacting George, really," Greta says sweetly as she saunters towards me.

Her whole attitude takes a one-eighty turn.

"Did you not miss me while I was away?" She is right in front of me now, her delicate manicured fingers unbuttoning the top button of my shirt.

"Of course, I did. That is not even a real question, is it?" I exhale reluctantly, her touch electrifying my senses.

"We brought her home, we fed her, we are giving her a safe place to stay for the night and a little excitement to top it all off. Trust me, she is one very happy girl right now. What young woman would not want a handsome stranger sweeping them off their feet in a foreign city? She is perfectly fine. I promise you." Her words are flowing over me, sedating me as with each syllable she utters she unfastens a new button.

"Now." She pushes the open shirt up and over my shoulders until it falls to the ground, "Do you not want to spend some time alone with me Mr. Anthony?" She lifts her smoky eyes up at me coyly.

"Of course, I do, Mrs. Anthony." I pull her into me by her soft thick hips.

"Then what I did, it's not so bad now, was it?" Greta says, knowing exactly what she is doing by slowly tracing her lower lip with the tip of her pointed nail.

I lean in and take that lower lip into my own two lips and hold it there, only releasing it long enough to say, "No, not at all. I am sorry my love."

Greta's hands clasp around the back of my head pulling it forward until our foreheads are touching, "Good. Now, take me to the bedroom, already won't you?"

As she commands I lift her up, her legs wrap around my waist securing me between them. She leans her head back fully revealing her immaculately round breasts as they try to break free from her dress. I dive my mouth into them, tasting each sweet inch as down the hall we slid until our bodies hit the bed in unison.

Even though Greta's homecoming has been marked with the same passion that has been the cornerstone of our relationship, I cannot sleep soundly tonight. I missed her while she was away. I am delighted for her to be home, lying naked next to me. I always sleep better just knowing she is near and safe. And yet tonight, the comfort of her hand resting on my bare chest is not soothing my anxiety. No, here I lay wide awake, my heart pounding out of my chest. Nessa has not returned from her date with Ansel and it is already half past one. What could they possibly be doing out this long? The answers to my own question only drive me crazier. I do not know what it is that has me spiraling out this way. I feel protective of her. It is almost as if she is somehow a piece of me.

I turn over and stare at the rose-colored Himalayan Salt lamp on the nightstand. Its gentle glow and low hum penetrate my mind and I am entranced by it.

"Nessa?" I can hardly believe the sight before my eyes.

"Oh shit, George! Hey!" She brightly confirms it is in fact her. Although the vision in front of me, trying unsuccessfully to hide the beer in her hand, barely resembles the girl next door. She is wearing fishnet stockings, leather military style boots, a shirt I can see her bra through, and her eyes are outlined with heavy black liner. But it is her unmistakable smile that gives her away, even swathed in blood-red lipstick.

"Georgey! Wish our girl a happy birthday!" Sami cuts in from behind Nessa. She is dressed almost identically, but uninhibitedly holding two large beers her hands.

"Happy Birthday!"

I feel incredibly awkward. I want to reach out and give her a hug. We have hugged before, but it suddenly does not feel the same.

"Sami got me the tickets to celebrate!" She is looking a bit nervous.

"Hell yeah, little Miss Nessa Reilly is eighteen now! She is going to throw her bra at Nikki Sixx!" Sami takes a large sip from the beer in her right hand. She clearly has no qualms about this situation at all.

"That is...Well...I hope he catches it." I give her a playful punch on the shoulder.

I hope he catches it? I am such a blockhead.

"Come on!" Sami pulls at Nessa's arm. "Iris and Cat are waiting at the front, we got to get up to them!" Sami starts walking away towards the growing crowd on the floor.

"Later!" Nessa yells as she starts off behind Sami. The crowd envelops them.

My stomach tightens until I see Nessa running back through the crowd toward me.

"Hey, my dad doesn't know I'm here. He'd totally freak." She looks sheepish, "Can this be our secret, please?" Nessa gives me a pleading look.

"Of course. Our secret." I wink at her.

"And, thank you. You may not remember, but you were the one who introduced me to Mötley Crüe."

And with that, she turns back into the sea of people. But not before she looks back, curves the right side of her lip up and waves at me.

A noise outside the window interrupts my reverie. Voices. Footsteps. My body reacts without so much as consulting my brain. I am up from the bed pulling on sweatpants and a t-shirt. I am down the hallway into the kitchen when I see Ansel and Nessa's shadows pass the living room windows. They are talking softly, intimately. I cannot make out what they are saying though. I inch in closer, trying to hear what is being said between them, but the front door opens. Shit! I scurry backward like a rat in an alley. I do not think they saw me. I lean further back into the hallway. Concentrating, I listen for more than one pair of footsteps, but I only hear her careful, but deliberate strides. My heart is pounding in fear and racing from excitement. For a moment I dare not move, unsure of what I should say or how it would look for me to be waiting up for her like this. But I have to see her. I swallow hard and step into the living room.

CHAPTER 10
A TAMBOURINE TYPE OF GIRL

The walk to the barman's apartment took only a few minutes and felt even quicker than that. I barely saw the way through the streams of silent tears. A few turns and a flight of stairs was all I could decipher. All the while he held me tight into his side whispering, "You're safe now, I've got you." He said it over and over again until I believed it.

Once inside his tiny flat, he locks the door behind us and sits me down on the tiny wine-colored love seat that sat against the interior wall. Without him attached to me, I shiver with cold, but he doesn't hesitate for a moment.

"Here, wrap this around you." He says placing a large, loosely woven blanket around my shoulders. It is heavy and warm and settles my nerves almost immediately.

"I'll put the kettle on, make some tea." He gestures toward the stove with his hands, clearly not sure exactly what to do with me.

"Tea sounds nice." My voice is much softer than it has ever been in my life. It feels like learning to speak for the first time.

"Milk and sugar alright?" He peers over from the kitchen.

The light in there is much brighter than where I am sitting. It glows over him. I nod my head in agreement as he goes about the preparations. It seems like quite a specific process.

As he goes about his work I look around the one room flat. The floors are a light-colored wood and creak a bit under your feet. The walls are white with a mint green trim and photos of guitarists decorate the blank spaces. The furniture is a mish-mosh of color and style. He clearly decorated it on a student's budget, but the place is immaculately clean. Even what I can see into the kitchen, the vinyl countertops are spotless. I don't know why, but the thought of him spending an afternoon cleaning brings a smile to my face.

"Glad to see that again." He says sweetly motioning to my mouth as he crosses the room to me.

He hands me my tea and takes a seat on the barstool that sits under the ledge separating the kitchen from the rest of the apartment.

"I don't even know your name." I think out loud as I watch him pick up his guitar.

"Aaron. You can call me, well...Aaron." He laughs nervously. "And you?"

"Sami, with an I not an MY. I guess we really didn't meet in any kind of traditional way." I say somewhat embarrassed.

"I don't know about that, some would say it's the most traditional way to meet someone." He picks up his guitar and starts strumming. It looks like second nature to him.

"How long have you been playing?" I ask.

"About ninety-seconds or so, give or take." He responds with all seriousness.

I giggle, "Sounds it." And his mouth gapes open.

"Oh, suppose I had that coming. I bought her at a flea market my first week here which was about two and a half years ago now. I've been teaching myself ever since." He looks down and continues to play a song that sounds familiar, but I can't quite make out.

I listen for a moment before asking, "Your guitar is a her?"

He looks up at me with a sparkle in his eye, "All great guitars are ladies. George Harrison had Lucy, Brian May has his Old Lady and BB King had Lucille."

"What is your girl's name?" I lean forward with curiosity.

"Sami with an I not an MY." He says not skipping a beat or losing the sparkle in his eye.

"Bullshit!" I sit back into the love seat and he begins playing again.

"Your right, that's a woeful name." He looks up at me again from the guitar, "Her name is Daisy."

"It suits her." I take a sip of my tea and listen on as Aaron begins softly singing.

"Blackbird singing in the dead of night. Take these broken wings and learn to fly. All your life. You were only waiting for this moment to arise."

I find myself so at ease, I start to sing along with him, "You were only waiting for this moment to arise. Blackbird fly into the light of a dark black night."

"That was lovely you have a very beautiful voice there. Here give her a try." He says jumping up and slinging the guitar across my lap.

"Me? No way, I have no clue what to do. I'm more a tambourine type of girl," I mutter nervously.

Laughing he positions himself over the edge of the loveseat so he is almost entirely behind me. "Just try." He folds his left hand around mine, gently placing my fingers on specific strings. His right arm grazes mine down from our shoulders to our hands and his thumb guides mine up and down. A shockingly melodious sound comes from the instrument.

"See you're a natural." He says, not taking his hands away

from mine. Together we continue to strum the same chord. After a few moments, he slides away from me, stands in front of where I am sitting and watches in delight at his very simple protégé.

"When do we go on tour?" I start strumming with comedically increased vigor.

Nervously laughing, Aaron slowly takes the guitar back and places it onto a stand. "More tea?"

"No. Thank you though. It was really nice of you to make me tea, and bring me here, and save me from that fucktard, and letting me moan on and on about Nessa. God, I must owe you a life debt by now." My head sinks into my hands in complete shame.

"You owe me nothing." He says sweetly and I peek out at him through my fingers.

"I am just so sorry I told you to wait outside for me and that guy...and he..." I hear the guilt building in Aaron's voice nearly choking him.

"It's not your fault." I cut him off.

I wrap the blanket tighter around my shoulders and let out an involuntary yawn.

"Do you want to stay here tonight? No funny business." He is completely transparent standing before me.

"Really?" I ask in disbelief despite his upright demeanor.

"You can have the bed and I'll sleep here on the sofa. It's not much in terms of size." He motions to the double bed in the corner, "But it is really comfortable and I have plenty of pillows." He looks like a little boy showing off his stuffed animals and it is the sweetest thing I think I have ever seen.

Unsure I say, "I don't have anything to wear." I don't know why I keep pushing back. I certainly don't want to go back to the hostel alone.

Sitting back down on the stool he says, "I have plenty of t-shirts and pajama pants. All clean, I promise."

"Why are you being so nice to me?" My inner monologue busting out of my mouth again.

"You remind me of my sister." He says without hesitation.

I feel my face drop, even though I try to hide my disappointment at his answer with all my might.

"Oh," I whisper.

Jumping back up to his feet he blurts, "I just mean that, if Bridget was alone in a strange city, a little emotional and sort of drunk-"

"I sound like a real winner." I interrupt his ramble.

"I would want someone to be nice to her and protect her no strings attached." He is standing absolutely still now in front of me.

Looking up at him, his dark eyes are locked on me, "You might be the best person I've ever met in my life." I tell him.

"I think that might be the Tequila talking." He breaks the tension with a joke.

"I'm completely sober now." I keep his gaze.

"Well then." He is stuck still where he stands. Then suddenly becoming very aware of himself he starts to stroll about the room, "Well um...save the sainthood for when I master that water into wine trick."

"You'd be the most popular barman in town." I slide up to the edge of the love seat matching his energy.

"I wouldn't be here anymore that's for sure." He says now back in the kitchen washing up the mugs from our tea.

"You don't like it here?" I ask moving across the room to meet him.

"It's complicated, I suppose." He pauses a moment to think. "I love my classes and I could see myself studying forever, the perennial student, ya know? I'm just tired of Berlin, I suppose. Tired of being away. God, that sounds awfully pretentious." He rolls his eyes at himself.

"Not at all." I assert.

"It's nothing against the city, it can be just wonderful. I guess I am just ready for things to be familiar again." He appears nostalgic while drying my mug with a navy-blue hand towel.

"I have only been away from home for a week and I feel that way, I can't even imagine two years," I admit, slightly embarrassed of my homesickness.

"It hasn't been all bad, don't get me wrong. I did a lot of traveling in the beginning. I would like to get back to that a bit before I go, see more of the world before fully graduating into adulthood as it were." His face lights up at the thought.

"Where will you go?" I lean towards him.

"Ah, everywhere." He laughs a deep laugh from the bottom of his throat. "Budapest, Copenhagen, Barcelona. Those are my top three anyway."

"So, go!" I cry out.

"Right now?" He mocks my misguided enthusiasm from earlier in the evening.

Raising an eyebrow at him I scold, "Very funny, mister."

"Sorry, it was just too adorable not to tease you." He playfully runs his hands through his trendy mop.

His compliment makes my stomach flutter and my cheeks blush.

"How much longer will you be here, in Berlin?" I ask wanting to know more about his plans.

He pops up onto the kitchen counter, sitting so casually next to the oven as we continue our conversation.

"A little over a year. I graduate September of next year." He says with tinges of both sadness and excitement.

"Then make the most of it!" I feign the enthusiasm he mocked me for just moments ago, but then more earnestly say, "Get out there! I'm jealous, I wish I was so close to everything, all of these jaw-dropping places. This is probably my one shot and it looks like I have totally blown it."

"It's not over yet, is it?" He asks.

"No, I guess not. Not until I find Nessa at least." I suddenly remember that I haven't heard a word from Nessa since our split. I am utterly bewildered by the situation I have found myself in.

"Then there is hope for both of us I'd say." His eyes are large, round, gentle and chipping away at my guard.

"Well, if I am going to stay here and I am not saying I'm going to yet..." I start.

"Right." He acknowledges my terms.

I continue, "Then we have to get to know each other better."

"Naturally. I'm a Sagittarius, devastatingly handsome and I enjoy long walks on the beach." He jumps in with his wry sense of humor.

"Are there many beaches in Berlin?" I ask suspiciously.

"None, actually." He shakes his head at me.

"Right. I think we should play the Zoo Game." I stare intently at him.

"The Zoo Game?" His eyebrows ask nearly as loud as his voice does.

"Yes," I say taking his hand and leading him to the love seat. "To get to know each other. You pick animals for your personal Zoo back and forth until our zoos are full."

"How is this getting to know each other?" He asks, though still holding firm to my hand as I lead him across the room.

I turn back to look at him as we reach the loveseat, "The animals a person picks says a lot about them."

"How big is the zoo?" He sits down next to me.

"As big as you want it to be. There are no limits in The Zoo Game." I cheerfully reply.

Leaning into me, "Does it have a sea life area?"

"If you want. No rules in the Zoo Game." I say, surprised

by how serious he is taking the game.

"And do I work at the Zoo?" He doesn't blink.

"Oh my god, you are mocking me, again aren't you?" I give a high-pitched squeak.

"Just a wee bit." He winks.

"There is no mocking in the Zoo Game." I lightly smack the back of his hand with mine.

"Very good. I'll be completely serious now." He takes my hand in his.

"Pick your first animal," I say with a rush of warmth from the intertwining of our hands.

He takes a moment to think, looking up at the ceiling.

"Lion." He states with the confidence of a king.

"A lion first, really?" I affect some deep insight, but his face drops.

"Is that bad?"

"No, not at all." I quickly assure him not wishing to break his spirit.

"And yours?" He squeezes my hand gently.

"Kangaroo," I answer in a second.

"Seriously? Of all the animals on earth, you pick the Kangaroo?" He genuinely asks.

"Have you ever seen a Kangaroo box? It would be like my own fluffy bodyguard!" I turn my body in to face him better.

"So, will my Lion." He retorts.

"Point taken." I motion for him to continue.

"Ok, second animal. I choose a shark." He is much more enthusiastic with his second choice.

"You've got a thing for predators." I give him a little poke.

"They should be respected." He pokes me back.

"Agreed. I pick a penguin." I say excitedly.

"Turtle." He continues.

"Parrot."

"Otter."

Our verbal tennis match is invigorating.

"Koala."

"Panda."

"Dog."

Our pace back and forth quickens to a fevered pace until he stops on his turn.

"You know, I'm happy with my animals. The zoo is closed."

"No more?" I am shocked by his abruptness.

"No, see I want to keep it small enough so I can give them all individual attention." He says sweetly.

"Cuddle time with the Great White?" I kid.

With one eyebrow up, he softly says, "He is a very tender beast." And I start to giggle.

"So, what did you glean from all this?" He asks, now back to his normal voice.

I speak very slowly, "I now know that you are a good enough a guy to go along with my silly games." My eyes scan back and forth for his reaction.

"You mean my animal combination hasn't given you some deeper insight into my psyche?" He is shocked at the realization.

"I'm not a psychologist. It is just some fun to pass the time." I wrap both my hands around his.

"I have to say, I'm a little disappointed." He says scrunching his face in sadness. "But it was fun." His scrunched face turns back into his signature wide smile.

"It was." My stomach flutters at his joy.

"So, will you stay?" His voice is full of hope.

I pause for a moment, even though I know what my answer will be.

"I think I will take you up on that bed now if that is okay?" Before I can finish my sentence, he has jumped up from the loveseat.

"More than okay!" He buzzes.

And with that, he is off and into the closet on the far side of the room. He pulls out some green flannel pajama pants and a plain grey t-shirt. He hands them to me gently. They are folded crisply and smell like fabric softener.

"Bathroom is right through there." He points to the cream painted wooden door next to the kitchen.

I stand up taking the pajamas from him. "Thank you."

Walking toward the bathroom I start to feel how extremely tired I am and how sore my body feels. My muscles are tight and stiff as if I've aged fifteen years in two hours. The bathroom is tiny and very European. It has pink rose walls, a sink you could barely fit both your hands into and a small stand up shower stall big enough just for one average sized adult. In the corner is a small wooden shelf stacked with bath towels. Suddenly a hot shower is the only thing on this earth I can think about. I open the frosted glass door, grab the twin silver handles, turn on the water as hot as it can go, slip off my clothes, and step in. The heat stings my body as the steam envelops me, holding me still. After a moment my body adjusts to the heat and I turn my back to the stream. The muscles in my back relax and expand. My shoulders lower and I take a deep breath, deeper than I have in what seems like forever. Dipping my head back gently I allow the water to flow through my hair. I take some of his body wash from the dark blue bottle on the white plastic caddy around the shower head. It smells sort of sweet and spicy. As I spread the gel over my body I wince. The lightest touch of my own hand causing me intense pain. It feels as though my skin is covered head to toe in bruises even though there are none to be seen. I quickly rinse off, wanting nothing more than to lie down and sleep. I open the fogged shower door and watch the steam billow out and fill the minuscule room.

"Sami," Aaron calls through the door.

I wrap a towel around my body and crack the door slightly to call back to him. "Sorry, I just saw the shower and I had to wash off."

"No, no, please don't worry. Whatever you need, it's yours. It's just your mobile is making some sort of chirping noise. I thought you'd want to know."

"It's chirping? It didn't play a song?" I ask shocked by what he is telling me.

"No just now, just a chirp like a small bird." His eyes don't drift down to my towel once.

"Damn it. Hold on." I close the door between us, slip the towel from my body to around my hair and pull on Aaron's pajama pants and t-shirt. I feel comforted by their softness and size. Swinging open the bathroom door, I beeline straight for my bag sitting on the coffee table and pull out my phone. My eyes drift for a moment to look up at Aaron who is carefully adding extra pillows and blankets to the bed.

"I have three voicemails. How is that even possible? I've been glued to my phone and I haven't gotten a single call." I press the phone directly into my ear not wanting to miss a word. Nessa's voice brings tears to my eyes, it is soft and sweet, but sad at the same time. As I listen from one message to the next, my jaw drops at what I am hearing. When they finish I just sit for a moment staring at the screen. I try dialing her back immediately, but it just rings and rings and rings. No answer, no voicemail box.

"Is everything alright?" Aaron asks hesitantly.

I inhale sharply, "I have no idea. She found him."

"George?" He blurts out.

"But, he's married." I look up at Aaron, my eyes wider than I ever thought they could possibly be. "And now, she bought us tickets to Spain."

"Things move very fast in your world, don't they?" He

asks moving back closer to me and sitting on the arm of the loveseat.

"I never used to think so." I shrug.

I try to dial her number again, but I get nothing. "The call still won't go through. I don't understand it." I well up with tears.

"Send her an SMS. Tell her you'll be there." He tries to comfort me.

"She hasn't responded to any of my text messages, I don't know if she is even getting them." A tear rolls down my cheek even though I am trying desperately to keep it together.

Aaron slides down the arm of the loveseat and puts his arm around me, "We have to hope for the best then."

I lean my head against his shoulder, "Thank you."

I type away to Nessa. A text message never felt more like a message in a bottle.

"So, you are leaving then?" He moves his arm to give me some space.

"Tomorrow." We meet eyes.

"Well then, you had better get a proper night's sleep young lady. We can't have you making a bad name for Canadians abroad, now can we?" He jumps up and offers me his hand.

"Death before dishonor." I take his hand and he helps pull me up off the loveseat.

The few short steps to the bed are filled with words neither of us say out loud. I slip under the covers, pulling them all the way up over my shoulders nearly to my mouth.

"Goodnight," Aaron says sweetly as he turns off the lights around the flat.

I watch his shadow travel across the room and lay down on the love seat. Then I can't fight it anymore. I close my eyes and fall fast asleep.

CHAPTER 11
GUILTY BY ASSOCIATION

Walking down George's street on Ansel's arm has to be the most surreal moment of my life. Here I am in a gorgeous foreign country, in a city I never thought I'd see in my life, having a first date with the brother of the wife of the man I'm truly in love with. It is all a bit too Maury Povich for me. But then I look at the street lights dancing through the trees, feel the soft breeze tickle my skin and hear Ansel gently humming "On the Street Where You Live" from My Fair Lady. It is a perfect moment, idyllic. To any stranger looking in, this would be a fairytale. I can see the fairytale, I can very nearly feel it, but it is as if a glass wall of my own design is keeping me from it. Why can't I just let it be mine? Maybe this is how it was always supposed to turn out. George isn't the one I am meant to be with, he is meant to connect me to the man I am meant to be with. Maybe I've been reading the signs wrong all this time. He is not my love, but merely a conduit for me to find love.

"Thank you again for a really nice night. It was wonderful, actually." I wrap my arm even farther through Ansel's. His muscular arm holds me there against his firm body.

Ansel leans his head down towards mine to answer. "It was truly my pleasure. I just hope I did not bore you too much with all the restaurant talk."

"Not at all. It was fascinating." It is only a baby lie that comes out of my mouth.

"You are too charming not to trust." His intimidatingly blue eyes stay fixed on me for a moment before I realize we are back in front of George and Greta's flat. The living room windows have gone dark since we left.

"What time is it?" I wonder aloud to Ansel.

"It is nearly two in the morning." He answers looking down at his white gold Rolex.

"Wow! The time really flew." I stop at the steps to the front door. Taking a small step up I am face to face with Ansel. He really is gorgeous. Chiseled features and perfect hair on a tall, muscular frame.

"Would it be too bold to kiss you good night?" He asks moving close to me and wrapping two of his fingers around just my right pinky.

Kiss him, kiss him, kiss him you idiot!

I am screaming inside.

"Ansel, you are a very sweet guy," I say, very stupidly not kissing him.

"Say no more." He takes a half step back.

"Sorry," I whisper placing my free hand on his chest. Really, I think I am just as disappointed as he is. There is just something deep inside telling me not to do it.

Ansel releases my pinky finger in exchange for taking both my hands in his. They are warm and enveloping.

"Never be sorry for knowing what you want." With that, he kisses my hands one at a time and steps away to leave.

I open the door as quietly as possible and look back. Ansel is waiting just a few steps away to make sure I get inside safely.

"Goodnight." I smile, still feeling somewhat apologetic.

"Goodnight, beautiful Nessa." He blows a kiss before walking away into the early morning.

I close the door, gently lock it and stay there for a moment watching Ansel walk away through the glass. I might just be the biggest idiot to ever live.

The apartment is dark, but it only takes a second for my eyes to adjust once I turn around from the door. I tiptoe over to the couch and pull my pajamas from my backpack. I slide the red flannel pants up under my dress and then pull the dress up over my head. Just before I slip my Black Sabbath t-shirt over my head I hear noise from the kitchen. My breath catches in my throat as I look over to see George. He looks like a deer in the headlights.

"Sorry, just wanted some water." He stutters barely finding the words.

We are both standing somewhat frozen in our spots looking at each other across the dark apartment. It is at this moment I become acutely aware of the fact I haven't put my t-shirt on yet. I've been standing here in just my pants and bra holding my shirt. No wonder George looks the way he does.

"Yea, yea. Sorry, I'll clean up this mess here." I turn my back to him, pull the shirt over my head and start stuffing everything else into my backpack. My cheeks are red hot.

"Please do not worry yourself, you are our guest." I still don't have the guts to turn back and look at him as he is talking to me. "Are you just getting in?" He continues.

"Yea, Ansel just dropped me off here a few minutes ago." I continue fiddling with my bag, keeping my back toward George until my awkwardness becomes less obvious on my face.

"Late night, huh?" I can hear that George's voice has moved closer, he is now in the living room with me.

"It was fun." I turn to see where he is and he is standing at the far side of the couch, a glass of water in each hand. It feels just the same as the night all those years ago when he cleaned up my knee.

"Fun?" He asks suspiciously.

"Don't worry, it was...completely innocent." I admit though I'm not sure exactly how much I should say. I take a seat at the edge of the couch.

George hands me a glass of water. "I was not trying to pry."

I give him a knowing look.

"Alright, fine maybe I was prying a little." He sits on the far side of the couch from me.

"Why?" I wonder.

"Ansel is a nice enough guy, but he is not for you." He answers with a certainty only found in men of a certain age.

"Why?" I push. Is there something he isn't telling me about the man who seems as close to Prince Charming as could be possible in reality.

"He is fine." George pauses, mouth open before finishing his thought, "You just deserve better."

"Better than a wealthy restaurateur?" I refuse to let the subject drop until George gives me something concrete. I mean a man with his own business that is pretty great.

"You know what I mean." I can see George starting to get flustered at my continued questioning.

"Do I?" I keep pushing him. Something about his attitude about Ansel really makes me want to dig in my heels.

George leans forward across the couch towards me slowly, deliberately. "You have an eyelash." He ever so gently presses his finger to my right cheek and pulls back for me to see the eyelash. "Make a wish." He prompts.

"I wouldn't know where to begin." For the first time since we saw each other again, I feel like I am back with George where we grew up. As if we are on his mother's couch and no time has passed at all. I close my eyes and lightly blow the hair from his finger.

"More water?" I open my eyes as George stands quickly moving back towards the kitchen.

"Wine?" I need something a little stronger than water, that's for sure.

"White?" He confirms.

"Yes please! Will you join me?" I cajole him.

"I, uh." He stammers.

"Come on! You sprung a blind date on me!" I'm sitting up on my legs and speaking as compellingly as I can without fear of waking Greta.

"That was not me!" George exclaims, shocked by the accusation.

"Guilty by association." I stand firm.

"That I am. Alright, you have twisted my arm." He pours two glasses and returns to the couch. Handing one glass to me, he once again takes a seat at the opposite side. "You are a very, very bad influence, Nessa Reilly."

I can't help, but giggle into my glass jetting the wine around, "That's a laugh coming from the original bad influence!"

"What do you mean the original bad influence?" George clearly surprised by my reaction.

"Oh, you don't remember the neighborhood block parties?" My eyes widen.

"A lifetime ago," George answers dismissively.

"Your parents would cook for days." I remind him.

"And yours would buy the liquor store out of stock." He replies.

"Yes, and there was always some kind of pranks or shenanigans going on and you were always the mastermind behind it. Like the time you mooned everyone from on top of the roof." He can't deny I am telling the truth.

"We sure did have fun back then." He laughs.

"How did we ever survive that three-ring circus?" I take a sip of my wine.

"You remember the circus?" He looks at me, shocked by the reference.

"Of course, I do. Do you?" The question comes out more pointed then I intend.

"Nessa, yes of course I do. We got out, just like you always wanted." George reaches out his glass to clink mine.

We both drink.

"Well some of us quicker than others." I push errant strands of hair from in front of my face.

George watches me for a moment, "So tell me about yourself."

What does that mean? He obviously already knows me.

"What about me?" I question him.

"Well to start with, where are you living? What are you doing? Do you still run around the old neighborhood in a zebra print onesie?" His eyes glimmer in his delight at teasing me.

"That was one time!" I squeal.

He continues on, "You came to my door."

"Stop!" I plead.

"In your pajamas." He pushes.

"Ah!" I sigh.

"In a ravishing shade of fuchsia glitter eyeshadow." He is completely straight-faced.

"Mortifying!" I dramatically hide my face in the couch cushion.

"Asking for a cup of sugar." He finishes his theatrical retelling.

I remove my face from the cushion to say, "It was my fourteenth birthday, we were playing truth or dare."

"It was pretty funny, that is for sure." He takes a sip of his wine.

"Well, thank you for not laughing in my face back then. I would have been crushed." I match his sip.

"I would not have dared. There was always something about you." He searches for the word he is looking for. "A bravado."

The wine catches in my throat, I've never been described that way in my life. "You make me sound like Clint Eastwood."

"A very sweet, very cute Clint Eastwood." He corrects me.

There it is. The word no woman hoping to be seen in a romantic light wants to be called.

"Cute," I repeat after him.

"Yes?" He looks confused.

"Right." Cute is the way he sees me. Like a bunny rabbit or a cartoon mouse.

"What is wrong? Are you saying you do not want to be a cute Clint? It is a compliment I assure you." He looks rather disappointed.

I better walk this back before I start saying what I am really thinking.

"No, of course, I do. Sorry, I'm just a little tired and getting a little tipsy." I explain apologetically.

George's eyes and lips narrow. I sense he doesn't really buy my line. He turns his body in more to face mine.

"Have you been writing?" He asks.

"Off and on." I deflect.

He doesn't allow for my vague response. "Why?"

"That's what I do. I'm a writer...or I'm trying to be." Trying is one way of putting it.

"I meant why off and on? Why not on and on? And on

and on and on and on and on." He rolls his head in dizzying circles.

Reaching out I grab his forearm to stop his momentum. "It doesn't pay the bills, let's put it that way."

"It should! It could! I know you!" His enthusiasm surprises me.

"I don't know about that." I pull back my hand looking down at my half empty glass of wine.

Reaching out and nudging my arm, George encourages, "You should not be so stingy with that brain of yours. The world could use a little piece."

"The world could use a little peace." I shoot him a wink and a peace sign with my fingers.

"I am being serious here." He has me locked in his stare. Even though they have lines at their corners, his eyes haven't aged a day.

I swirl my wine in its glass, "Me too."

"Nessa, what is really going on? How did I find you crying in a German airport? What are you doing wandering aimlessly through Europe? Why are you not holed up in a little flat surrounded by books and a shaggy dog and a bottle of whiskey like a proper writer?"

"Now you are a comedian?" I ask though there is not a shred of a joke behind his words now.

"I am just trying to figure out why the girl who wanted to set the world on fire seems to be letting her embers fade." He is relentless.

"Because nobody wants me! Nobody wants my manuscripts. Nobody wants a piece of my brain. I'm single, I sling drinks and tacky entrees and that is all there is to me. Nobody cares what I have to say. Nobody wants me, okay?"

I'm out of breath.

"I want you!" George quickly blurts out.

We are both stunned into silence by our words. We sit in it for a moment. Not really knowing how to continue.

Quietly I start, "Sometimes I feel like I am writing the same story over and over again hoping that the ending will be different."

"You are the writer; can you not just change it? Write the ending that you want." George's voice is much gentler now.

"I tried, but maybe it's just not for me. I mean one hundred rejection letters should tell me that, right?" I shake my head.

"Hey," He places his hand on my knee squeezing it gently. "I believe in you."

"Do you really?" I wonder out loud.

"Of course, I do. I always have." His hand is still on my knee.

"That means a lot to me." I suddenly feel like crying, but I hold it in.

"I should not be keeping you up so late. I am sorry." George moves his hand back to his lap, sitting up straight as though he might stand.

"Don't be silly. I've enjoyed it." I softly say.

"Me too." He leans forward pushing up to his feet.

"Do you remember the last time we stayed up late talking like this?" I ask hoping he'll stay a little longer.

He turns his head to look at me, "It has been a very long time."

"Seven years ago. You were visiting your parents the summer after you moved to Seattle." My eyes stay locked in on him looking for some recognition of the memory.

"And I quite drunkenly lost my keys." He sits back down and leans into a more comfortable position on the couch. "I was lucky you were going through your insomniac phase or I would have had a very uncomfortable sleep on the stoop."

My stomach leaps at his reaction. "Well, I'm not sure you

were that much more comfortable with the Pimp My Ride marathon."

George smiles at the thought, "You were great company then and you still are. You never did say, where are you living now?"

"I'm still in D.C. I have a little studio in the Cleveland Park area." I cross my legs in towards George.

"And are you happy?" He asks, but I want to return to what we had just been talking about.

"Do you remember anything else from that night?" I pry gently.

"You mean convincing your dad I was up early to deliver the paper?" He laughs.

But I continue on, "Before that."

"Uh, I do not think so?" He says slowly.

"Doesn't matter." I quickly finish my glass of wine. This was a mistake.

"What? Tell me what is swirling around up there." He points to the side of my head.

Don't do it. Don't say it, Nessa. Just leave it alone.

Danger, danger, danger.

"Ok, this is going to sound a bit crazy..." Oh boy, the warnings didn't work. "But I thought there was a moment that night where we..."

"Almost kissed?" He finishes my sentence.

"Yes," I say breathlessly. He knew exactly what I was thinking.

"You do not sound crazy." George looks deep into my eyes and for a moment we are back there on my parents' couch at four in the morning. We are just inches apart. I want to kiss him. I want to make up for the moment that we missed out on. I want to put my hands on his firm chest and softly press my lips to his. I want us to share the same air. And for a moment I think he wants me too.

But then I remember Greta is only a few feet away, sleeping soundly, completely unaware of my intentions here with her husband.

"We should both get some sleep," I say with the greatest amount of sadness I think I've ever felt.

I uncross my legs and move forward on the couch to sit up straight.

"Did I say something wrong?" George asks nervously.

"No! No, I am...exhausted. This wine has gone straight to my head. I just want to lay down." I try to quickly escape his concern.

"I can only imagine how exhausted you are. Have you heard anything from Sami?" He takes the empty wine glass from my hand before standing.

"No, nothing yet." A new, different wave of sadness hits me.

"Can I convince you to stay a day or two more? Sami is welcome to join you here as well. It has been so great seeing you and Greta really wants to get to know you. You girls can spend a few days with us, it will be like old times." His genuine sweetness is shining through the darkness of the room.

"Your offer is too kind. Greta is lovely and you are a beautiful couple. I am really, truly happy for you both. I think though, I have to go. I have to go to Sami, find her and apologize." I say firmly.

"Well, I will drive you to the airport tomorrow morning then." George walks the glasses to the kitchen and places them quietly in the sink.

"That will be nice. Thank you." I force a smile.

George starts walking in toward the direction of his bedroom. "Sleep tight."

"Don't let the bed bugs bite," I call after him.

He stops to look back at me, "You still have that same cock-eyed smile."

"I've missed you too." We share a moment and he continues down the hall.

A few seconds pass and I hear the bedroom door close with a light thud.

I feel lighter, empty, like a fraction of myself. I feel like a weight has been taken off my shoulders or more accurately like a cannonball blew straight through the center of my body leaving a gaping hole.

I lay down on the overstuffed, cashmere covered couch by curling into a ball. I reach into my bag and hit Sami's number on my phone.

Sami, please answer.

Voicemail again. Damn it.

I don't know what to do with myself. I want to run. I want to cry. I want to scream. Usually, when I feel like this I pop in my headphones and take a long walk around the city. The passing faces moving in time to the sounds of Queen is a sure-fire way to pull me back from the edge. I pull my laptop from my bag. I have to make the big gesture here. I have to win my best friend back. Sami has been talking about Spain since we saw the movie Vicky Christina Barcelona. Perfect. There are flights that will get us both there around the same time tomorrow morning. I book them and grab my phone. Sami's phone rings and rings and rings. No answer. So, I lay it all out there and hope she hears it.

It's now three in the morning. I'm tired, totally exhausted physically, mentally and emotionally. Sami and I have been separated for eighteen hours. I haven't seen or heard from her. I am terrified something has happened to her. The worst possible scenarios are playing on repeat in my head. I am hoping upon hope that she isn't ignoring me and making me suffer on purpose, but I can't say I would blame her if she was.

Eighteen hours...now nineteen hours.

I lay still as the dead staring at my phone waiting for it to ring, light up or chirp...waiting for any sign of life. But as I stare at the glowing brick in my hand I can feel my eyes grow heavier. I fight it.

"Nessa...Nessa wake up." I hear a familiar voice through a very foggy sleep. I hear it, but I can't seem to open my eyes to answer it.

"Nessa." This time the voice comes with a pleading shake to my arm. I open my eyes to see George crouched in the dark next to my face. Jumping up with a gasp I nearly knock him back off of his feet and on to the floor. My eyes now open painfully wide to take in the nearly black room. My eyes dart from the couch to the window, to the kitchen. It takes me a moment to remember where I am. The apartment is dark, no one else is around. I couldn't have been asleep for more than a few minutes. My eyes finally focus on George who is still bent down in front of me.

"What's wrong? What's going on?" I asked feeling the panic build inside me as the questions leave my mouth.

George takes a seat next to me on the couch not yet saying a word.

I push up on my arms so I am sitting.

"Did Sami call? Is she in trouble?" I feel on the verge of hysteria.

"No." George breaks his silence while taking my hands in his.

I look down at our hands intertwined, trying desperately to make my brain process faster.

"I just needed to do this."

My eyes are still looking down into his hands when I feel his face brush mine and our lips touch. It's slow and soft. It's not how I imagined it at all. His hands aren't in my hair or wrapped around my face in a passionate embrace the way you see in all romantic comedies. It's not even the way I saw it in my dreams. We stay there for a moment, not even breathing as the delicate skin of our lips come together. Our muscles relax. I ever so gently part my lips inviting him in further. His hands' release mine as our lips sink deeper into each other and he wraps his arms around me. He dips me back down on to the plush oversized throw pillows and there we are making out on the couch in the dark like a couple of teenagers. It is light and exciting and fun. I feel as though I could float right up and into the atmosphere. The euphoria of it all is intoxicating.

"Nessa?" George's deep melodious baritone whispers my name.

"Yes." I try to reply, but my mouth is still on his. We haven't stopped kissing since we began.

"Nessa?" He calls again, but how? What strange ventriloquism. I open my eyes to look for him, but the eyes above me staring back into mine are not his at all.

"Nessa!" This time he shouts and I realize the voice is coming from next to me, not above. I turn my head to the side and see George standing like a tower over me. I turn back looking for the lips I've been kissing to find Greta smiling her sickeningly perfect smile back at me.

"She is not even a good kisser, darling." Greta divulges to George as she stares down at me. I feel like a rabbit under a rattle snake's gaze. She leans her head down toward my face. I can't tell if it is to either kiss or devour me whole. I try to push her away, but I feel weak. I try to scream, but no voice appears. I look to George for help but he is gone.

Bang!

I wheeze for air. I can hardly get enough no matter how hard I try. I open my eyes carefully afraid of what I might see, but there is no one there. I am alone. It was just a dream. Drenched in sweat I feel such a deep sense of dread. I search for my phone only to realize the crash that woke me from my nightmare was my cell phone dropping from my hand to the rich wooden floor beneath me.

I pick it up to place it under my pillow, but when I see it I nearly scream. A tiny, green box on the center of the screen with SAMI in bold black type inside of it. She wrote me a text! I open it up and it says "I'll be there. I'll see you in Barcelona first thing tomorrow. I love you!"

I have to go. For so many reasons I have to get out of this apartment right away.

CHAPTER 12
A NOTE NOTHING MORE

The light from the sun is only barely brightening the night sky into day. There is just the vaguest twinkle of sunlight through the skylight in the ceiling. My eyes are only slits, but I can still see stars straight above me. Have I even slept at all? I do not know how I possibly could have. I close my eyes again, but all that is there is Nessa's face. Her wonderful, beautiful face smiling wryly back at me. Giving me that look she gives, the one where she is clearly reading my mind but is too sweet to say so. The look that causes me to inhale and laugh simultaneously. The look that brings me home again after all these years. I open my eyes again not just wanting to see her in my mind's eye. I want to see her in front of me living in the same space and breathing the same air. I want to hold her in my arms. I jump up out of bed not wanting to waste a moment of the time we have left together. Maybe she will even decide to stay longer. I have to tell her she can. I reach over into my bottom dresser drawer grabbing the first pair of jeans I can get my hands on. Sliding the dark blue denim up I hop over to the open closet to grab a shirt. Greta must have an early meeting today as I can see she has already torn through her side of the closet and left a trail of shoes across the room to the door. I am out the door and halfway down the hallway before I can get the plain white t-shirt over my head. I run through it all in my head.

"Nessa, I really think you stay until you hear from Sami. It is not safe to just go off on your own again. You have barely even seen Munich. At least spend some time taking in the sights. I could take you, show you around. I actually have tickets to Iron Maiden tomorrow night; would you want to join me?"

I am such an idiot. All I have to do is ask her and it will be a yes or a no and whichever it is we will all move on with our lives accordingly. There is nothing to stress out about. I have certainly dealt with more high-pressure situations than this. One girl, no, one woman cannot possibly unravel me. But nevertheless, my legs feel weak as I take one step after another down the hallway.

"Guten Morgen my love." Greta buzzes around the kitchen like a hummingbird. Tea in hand, makeup painted on and not a hair out of place. She is the Good Housekeeping magazine advertisement for the perfect wife.

"Guten Morgen." I turn left toward the living room to wish Nessa a good morning, but she is not there. Her things are gone and the couch sits as if no one even slept there. It is as if she was never here at all and the last twenty-four hours was a dream. But they were not a dream, they were so fantastically real. We sat just there, our bodies nearly touching, talking and laughing. I feel a cold sadness fall over me, like winter back home in Pennsylvania.

"Where is Nessa?" I question as calmly as I possibly can.

"She left," Greta says nonchalantly. As if I was already supposed to know. As if this is some predetermined fact.

I stare at her a moment, unable to put my thoughts together. "I was supposed to drive her to the airport," I respond, though it clearly means nothing in light of the situation.

And still Greta does not stop moving about the apartment, "She said she didn't want to be a bother, she had already called for the taxi by the time I was awake."

"She should not have done that. Why did you not wake me to tell me she was leaving so I could say goodbye." Gravity pulls me down to the couch, sitting where not even four hours ago I sat with her.

I lay my head back suddenly feeling the effects of the hangover from the late night and the wine.

"She told me not to. I must have startled her being up so early." Greta interrupts my self-loathing.

"Why do you say that?" I shift my head only slightly to catch her eye. She is now still, standing against the counter in the kitchen watching me.

"She left a note for us." I watch as Greta walks slowly, purposefully toward me. Her arm outstretched, the note dangles on the end of her fingers like a Christmas bulb on a tree. "I do not think she wanted to say goodbye." She almost looks as sad as I feel.

I unfold the slice of notebook paper and quietly read what Nessa has written. I hear her voice so clearly in my head.

"Dear George and Greta, thank you for your kindness. I'm certain I won't soon forget this night and how you both took me in when I was all alone. I wish you all the best. Hopefully, our paths cross again under the big top."

I cannot help but laugh. Under the big top.

"Strange behavior, don't you think?" I realize Greta has been standing over me as I read the note.

I quickly fold the note back up, "Nessa is always two steps ahead of everyone else, I am sure she had a good reason for this."

Greta takes the note from my hand and moves back towards the kitchen, "She is a very odd girl, though isn't she?"

"What do you mean?" I hop up from the couch and follow her into the kitchen for a cup of coffee and to see what she is going to do with the handwritten note.

"What I mean is that she is traveling all over Europe with no plan to speak of. She has no boyfriend at her age and she was not at all interested in Ansel. It just makes no sense to me." Greta's nonchalance digs under my skin.

"She told you that?" I quickly interject.

"No, of course not." Greta turns to look at me as I pour my coffee. "Ansel told me. He showed her a perfectly lovely night. He treated her to the very best and she would not even kiss him good night." Her tone is indignant at best.

"Well, she is not the kind of girl to be bought. She has her own mind and her own plans. I respect that." And then there was a silence so loud it could have deafened half of Munich.

"I just mean." I try but it is too late.

"Unlike me, you mean." Greta is scarily still, quietly cutting me off.

"Greta." I take a step towards her.

"Unlike me, you mean. She has a mind and I do not." Her eyes have not moved off of me once.

I take another step toward her, "Do not start this again, Greta."

"Start what George? Telling the truth?" Her eyes have widened and I can tell by that look I should not move any closer to her.

"The truth?" I asked buying myself some time.

"You don't see me as your equal. You never have." And with that, she is across the room angrily straightening pillows on the couch where I sat. Her go-to angry activity is always cleaning.

"Do not talk crazy, Greta." I stay put in the kitchen to avoid escalating the situation.

"See! Crazy! You think I'm crazy." She has now moved on to folding the throw blankets that hang over the matching armchairs.

"I do not think you are crazy. I think this conversation is crazy." I say as slowly and in as neutral a voice as I can.

She is moving about the room like a whirling dervish. "I don't have as much education as you. I don't have a prestigious job like you."

"If you do not like your job anymore then leave it." I take a small step around the counter toward the living room.

"Oh, so you can support both of us? I guess I'm just the kind of girl who can be bought though, right?" She yells, standing dead still in the middle of the living room.

"I never said that!" I cannot help but match her tone and volume.

"You didn't have to." She crosses past me, yelling in my face before moving back into the kitchen.

There is something about her getting so close and speaking so scathingly that boils my blood and I lose it.

"What do you want from me here? I married you. I am trying my damnedest to make you happy! For fuck's sake! Do you think I would still be here if not for you?"

She turns around to look at me. I can see the tears welling in her beautiful almond eyes and I am gutted.

"I love you, but I feel like I am constantly living on the edge of a broken heart." Her voice is now soft and almost childlike.

I feel defeated, "I have done nothing but be supportive of you, give you everything that you want. I do not deserve that."

"You just don't get it." She shakes her head.

"Explain it to me, Greta! What more can I give you?" I plead with her.

"Nothing!" She throws her hands up. "Forget it!" She slams her mug of tea into the sink and takes off for the door.

"Right just storm out," I yell after her.

"I have to go to work." She turns on a dime at me.

I am at a loss for words because I do not want to continue fighting. "See you later?"

"Sure." She says tersely as she turns again to leave.

"Greta." I follow her.

"What?" She asks without even turning around to look at me.

"Come here," I say softly.

She turns slowly towards me. "I have to go."

"Just come here, one second." I hold my arms open to her. After a moment of her staring me down, clearly weighing her options she walks into me. Her arms wrap fully around my waist and I fold mine around her back pulling her close to me. I rest my head on top of hers and the smell of her vanilla and patchouli perfume acts as a sedative.

"I'm sorry." She coos from beneath my arms.

"Shhhh." I pull her closer. "I can stop by the market and make us a nice dinner tonight. Would you like that?"

She pulls her head back to look up at me. "You are going to make dinner?"

"It is not so preposterous." I smile down at her.

She laughs. "What are you going to make?"

I kiss her forehead, "Steak, maybe some Schnitzel. Whatever you want."

"A steak would be divine." She kisses me gently.

I wish I could hold on to this moment, this love and contentment we are feeling right now. I tell her, "I love you."

Her eyes open up, "I love you too," and she squeezes me

closer. "But I do really have to go or I will be late to my meeting."

"Alright," I give her another kiss and let her go. Before she reaches the door though I cannot help myself but ask, "Did Nessa leave a number with you?"

"No. Why, did she forget something?" Greta asks so sweetly.

"I was just curious. I want her to be safe." I try to retreat from the conversation.

"It's kind of you to worry about her." Greta looks back and blows me a kiss before closing the door.

I watch Greta pass by the living room windows and I sink back into the couch. I open Nessa's note which I slyly placed in my jean's pocket while Greta was angry cleaning. I read it over again.

"Hopefully our paths cross again under the big top."

Her voice rings in my ears as I trace her handwriting with my thumb. I cannot understand why I am feeling this way. I miss her, deeply. It is not rational. My logical brain knows she has not been in my life for years. We are nearly strangers at this point. She was never supposed to be here. Finding her was a fluke. And now she is gone and life will go on the way it was always supposed to. I was happy enough and I will feel that way again.

Leaning my head back onto the couch my eyes close and the exhaustion from my lack of sleep washes over me. I sit here for a moment allowing myself to enjoy the rest. As my body relaxes my mind wanders back to that day. The last time I saw Nessa all those years ago. It was not that morning on the couch she remembers and running out the door once her dad woke up. That was the last time she saw me, but not the last time that I saw her. That moment came later.

The morning air is surprisingly chilly for August. The autumn seems to be arriving earlier and earlier with each passing year. The sun is just peaking over the church steeple on the corner of the street, leaving the houses below it shadowed in varying shades of cement. I did not turn my head even slightly to look into the Reilly's bay window as I passed it. I crossed the porch, ran down the steps and made the sharp turn back to my house. By now, surely mom is up and watching the news from Greece. I sheepishly knock on the door, trying only to be loud enough to be heard by her and not by my sleeping father. I waited holding my breath, praying none of the other neighbors are up this early. No answer. I knock again and look back at the Reilly's house, still not certain Mr. Reilly will not follow me out here for questioning...or worse. Before I can knock a third time I hear the door being unlocked. Sliding lock first, knob lock second and finally the door jamb is removed. My mom is in her nightgown wearing a look as though I might be the second coming of Jesus knocking at her door. Seeing me rather than Christ in front of her, disheveled, smelling of booze and bags under my eyes all she does is smack her tongue off the roof of her mouth in disgust and turn back into the living room. The house is warm as I step inside locking the door behind me. The newscaster's annoyingly nasal voice washes over me as I pass through the living room.

"Love you ma," I call down to her as I start up what seems like an endless mountain of stairs.

As soon as I reach my room I fall onto the bed, I do not even bother to get undressed. I should have kissed her. I replay the moment in my head. Both of us sitting there on her couch in the dark trying to stifle our laughter and she playfully smacks my leg with her hand. But before she can pull her hand back, I enfold my hand over hers and hold it for a moment. The feeling is electric. I turn my head to look at her and find myself caught in her green eyes. She is unwavering in her stare, the light from the television illuminates her freckles and the right side of her mouth is lifted into a cheeky half smile. All I want to do is kiss her, take her adorable face in my hands and feel her lips touch mine. We are both frozen, breathing in the moment, but I cannot do it. She is only nineteen and I am leaving in a few hours to go back to Seattle for at least six to ten months. I cannot, I will not do that to her, to either of us. I pull my hand back to break our gaze.

"Now, who really needs a hot tub in their van?" I point at the television and without skipping a beat Nessa jumps in.

"No one. It actually seems pretty reckless but that is the beauty of the show!"

It was then we heard the creak of her dad coming down the steps and we both shot towards the front door.

I should have kissed her. I close my eyes. I should have kissed her.

"George...George...It is the afternoon." A deep, gruff voice pulls me out of a restless sleep. "George!"

"Yeah, pop! I am getting up now." I roll over to face my dad standing in the cracked open door. He is still as a statue watching me with one eyebrow raised.

He speaks softly, slowly and menacingly. "Your mother is already a mess because you are leaving today for god knows how long and you decide to stay out all night with those idiot boys from up the street? Wake up, come downstairs, and have breakfast with your mother. She has been cooking all morning." And with that he is gone, he disappears from the door.

Breakfast, albeit a little late in the afternoon, flies by in a blink. I say goodbye to my father with a handshake and kiss my mother's tear-stained face. I throw my bag into the back seat of my silver Toyota Camry, but before I lean into the driver's seat I examine the Reilly's house for any sign of Nessa. It is quiet, all the doors closed and no sign of her anywhere. One last stop before I leave town, Barnes and

Noble® to pick up "The Heroin Diaries" on audiobook for the drive and a very large, very strong coffee.

Barely even a step through the door I am stopped dead in my tracks. It is her laugh. I would know it anywhere. She sounds like Betty Rubble come to life. Her lips locked together in a wide smile, her eyes sparkling with joy. I slowly walk the aisles hoping to find her reading in a corner. I follow the sound of her laugh. A high pitched "hmm hmm mmm mmm mmm." It is infectious. My stomach is turning at the prospect of seeing her. Should I kiss her now? Is the moment gone? Should I tell her I wanted to kiss her and at hearing that she will, in turn, kiss me? Maybe instead I should ask to kiss her. But we should not kiss in public like this, should we? Her warm giggle fills my ears. I turn the corner and there she is, sitting at a table in the café. Mojo magazine in one hand and an oversized white mug in the other. Her red hair is falling like delicate strands of ivy around her cherub-esque cheeks. I stand there in awe of her for a moment, gathering the courage to approach the table and sit beside her. And in that millisecond of hesitation, Eric swoops past her and plops down in the chair that was meant for me. He throws his arm around her pulling her into him. She grabs his t-shirt and kisses him, a passionate, meaningful kiss. So, I turn around and walk away. I walk straight out of the store without thinking twice about what I came for. I was never supposed to kiss her.

CHAPTER 13

KNOCK KNOCK...WHO'S THERE?

The night is sticky hot, but the swirling of the ceiling fan is keeping us cool as we sing and sway to the music. There is an electricity in the air here. I could feel it the moment I got off the plane, even before Nessa ran through the crowd to hug me so hard we both ended up on the floor. Even before Aaron texted me to say he was coming to Barcelona to meet us, I felt something here. I don't usually subscribe to such ideas, but if there were ever a place to have magic woven into its fabric this would be it.

"Alright, alright! I'm getting us another bottle, a pack of cigs and what else?" Aaron calls cheekily from just outside the poorly painted, poorly constructed hostel room door.

"Cherries!" Nessa and I call back in unison as we both jockey for position in the very tiny mirror over the sink.

"Where am I supposed to find cherries at this hour?" He retorts, his delicious accent on full display.

"This is Barcelona!" Nessa turns with the swing of her hip and the biggest smile I have seen her wear in years.

Aaron squints his eyes and with the tilt of his head asks,

"You do know Barcelona and Candyland are not one in the same, right?"

I catch his eye through the mirror and he flashes me a toothy grin. He looks incredible standing ever so nonchalantly, leaning against the door frame.

I cross the room to him, very aware of him watching me in my little black dress and heels. It is a far cry from how I looked when we first met. And even though I feel much more confident and in control now, he looks at me with the same sweetness as he did last night.

"There is a guy selling them down on the corner to the left. We met him earlier." I pat him on the chest, turning him around and out the door.

"I missed all the action it seems." He laments as I playfully give him a push

But as he briskly walks down the long hallway to the stairs I call out, "The night is still young!"

He turns back with a robotic flair, "I'll be back!"

I close the door behind me to see Nessa fully facing me with a cocky smirk on her face.

"You are such a smitten kitten!" Her expressive eyes glowing in gold shimmer eyeshadow.

"Shush you!" I feel my cheeks flush as I rejoin her in the mirror.

"Yes!" Nessa runs to her laptop and turns the volume all the way up as our favorite Gloria Estefan song hits the playlist.

"Sí seor, sí seor!" We sing along with Gloria.

I watch as Nessa dances in front of the mirror, swinging her silver mini-dress through the air. "You look absolutely fucking alive right now."

She gives me a squeeze. "I feel alive. I feel happy, finally! I went through all of the other feelings already. I was confused, angry, sad and I mean really sad. Now...I feel good baby!" She takes a drink of wine from her glass. "And now, I want to party with the fine people of Spain!" She ends with a twirl and shouts into the air.

Knock. Knock. Knock. Knock.

A firm pounding on the door catches us both off guard and sends us into a fit of laughter.

"What did you forget?" I holler out from across the room as I make my way to let Aaron back in.

I swing the door open only to see it is not Aaron at all. The man is facing away, looking down the hall. My heart catches in my throat. I slam the door shut and throw on the puny chain.

"No habla espaol!" I shout through the door.

"What is going on? Who is it?" Nessa asks in a drunken whisper.

"I don't know. Not Aaron though. It's a big guy with dark hair. Maybe he's like hostel security or something and he's come to kick us out." I look over to the bed where she is sitting.

"Were we being too loud?" Nessa shrinks.

I peak through the peephole, but it's too dirty to actually see through.

Knock. Knock. Knock. Knock.

"You have the wrong room," I yell through the crack in the door.

"Sami, open the door." A deep voice comes from the other side of the door.

Holy shit. Nessa and I look at each other, shocked.

I try again to look through the very dirty peephole, but to no avail. "How do you know my name?"

"Because I know you Sami and even if I did not, you just told me what your name was by your answer." The voice ends with an odd laugh. It is almost familiar.

"Oh my god." Nessa stands up from the bed her face white as a ghost.

"Ciao, creep!" I yell through the door.

"Sami, stop. That laugh." Nessa's eyes are glazed over.

Knock. Knock. Knock. Knock.

"Oh shit!" Nessa and I both swallow hard, realizing exactly who was on the other side of the door.

"Sami, please open the door. It is George. I am here to see Nessa." His voice still firm, but imploring.

Nessa runs past me and opens the door so quickly, I fear that it may come straight off its latches. "George?!"

All of the air is sucked out of the room.

She looks as though she didn't truly believe it was him until she saw his face. "What are you doing here?"

I hear the trembling in her voice, watch her hands grasp the door frame and I instinctually go to her. I stand directly behind her, place my hand on her shoulder and fix George with my most withering stare.

"Harassing young women in Catalan hostels obviously." He plays off the question with a joke.

"George, what are you doing here?" Nessa asks again, now much more confidently. I feel it in her posture beneath my hand.

George turns his body back, looking down the hall and then turns back to us, "It seems I'm interrupting girl's night. I will just leave."

He only takes one step backward when Nessa stops him with, "Wait!"

She breaks from my grasp and steps out into the hall, "You came all the way to Spain to knock on my door and then run away? Where is Greta?"

I step out with Nessa because I would very much like to know that answer as well.

"She is at home..." He trails off, picking his words extremely carefully. "She does not know I am here."

I look to Nessa for her reaction, but she is stone-faced and silent.

"God, you are gorgeous." George shatters the silence into a million pieces.

Nessa taps my leg with her hand, discreetly asking me to give them some privacy. I step slowly back into the room, close the door just enough without actually shutting it and listen.

"You left without even saying goodbye," George says sadly, his voice almost boyish in its innocence.

"I didn't want to bother you," Nessa responds stoically, but she barely finishes her sentence before George chimes in.

"Bullshit!" His voice noticeably less innocent than before.

"Fine! I didn't want to see you!" She raises her voice.

And I can feel the truth canoe tipping over the edge of the waterfall. I grab my purse and open the door. They both look at me sharply.

"You know what sweetie, we will be downstairs at the bar next door. The one with all the candles. You know the one?"

I kiss her on the cheek and she grabs my hand firmly. "Yes. Thank you."

At the top of the staircase I stop for a moment to listen if they've continued their conversation, but I don't hear anything. Then I smile, hearing Aaron singing to himself from below. He is dancing up the stairs with arms full of cherries and wine.

"Hello!" I smile down at him.

"That cherry man is just delightful! I bought two bags!" Aaron dances up to me.

I grab him by the shoulders and turn him back around on the stairs.

"What? Where are we going?" He asks, utterly confused.

"Out!" I sling my arm through his grabbing the pack of cigarettes from him.

"What about Nessa?" He asks while we walk carefully back down the steps.

"George showed up," I say with a look to him.

Aaron stops in his tracks, "The George? I want to get a look at him!" He turns to go back up the steps.

I grab a hold of his arm, "How about we share those cherries on the bench out front, watch the people pass by and if you're lucky maybe I'll show you a trick I can do with the stems."

"You drive a hard bargain, my dear girl." He leans in, "Lead the way."

CHAPTER 14
A DIFFERENT KIND OF DREAM

"Yes. Thank you." I grab Sami's hand as she pulls her face back from mine after giving me a meaningful kiss on the cheek.

I hear her tall, glittery heels carry her down the hallway, leaving only George and myself standing the in the poorly lit hallway. We are completely silent, not talking or taking our eyes off each other.

In fact, neither of us have said another word to each other since she opened the door, even while she kissed me goodbye, my eyes were on him. How different and yet how similar is the man I see in front of me, in comparison to the man I first fell in love with all those years ago on a dark December night. I can feel his eyes on my face, but I can't help but inspect him from the soles of his shoes upward. He stands with his left leg slightly forward out towards me, but his weight is resting back on his right leg. His jeans are slightly crumpled where they meet his slick chocolate brown shoes. A soft blue button-up shirt is rolled at the sleeves to reveal thick brown, nearly black arm hair. The raw masculinity of the image causes me to catch my breath. Looking up, a black undershirt peeks out from where he left the top buttons undone. His hair is much shorter than what I had remembered in my mind's eye. His lips are full, soft and tan. The permanent five o'clock shadow around his cleft chin and square jaw call out to me. It is telling me to grab him, kiss him and not let another opportunity slide through my fingertips.

When my eyes finally reach his, he is already there. He is unshaken, steady as always and refusing to let my gaze go.

"Why would you not want to see me?" He sounds hurt.

The emotion in his question catches in my throat.

"Just stop, please," I beg, still not breaking our eye contact.

He leans forward shifting his weight closer to me, "And what about what you wrote in your note?"

"What about it?" I shake my head dismissively.

He pulls out the small piece of paper I folded so carefully little more than twelve hours ago. "Under the big top."

"They are just words." The lie tears my eyes away from his.

"We both know that is not true." He reaches out taking my arm in his strong hand.

The contact forces me to look up at him and face the lies coming inexplicably from my mouth.

"George, I think you should go." I take a step back, releasing myself from him.

"Nessa." George's eyes match his piteous tone.

I don't know what to do. I absolutely do not know what to do here. I want to cry, and scream, and dance, and throw myself onto him all at once. And it is really fucking with my head. All of my dreams start replaying in rapid succession until I feel nauseous from the tilt-a-whirl movie in my head.

My hands grab the door frame and the door to steady myself, "George, you can't just show up at my door and tell me I'm gorgeous."

But before I can continue, George steps in so close our bodies are almost touching. He takes my face into my large hands and kisses me. And in that single moment, time stops completely.

George pulls back slightly, his hands still draped just below my ears. His lips are barely separated from mine as we both open our eyes.

I take my hands off of the door frame even though I am sure doing so will cause me to fall off the earth.

I envelop my fingers over George's hands bringing them down between us.

"My life isn't a Julia Roberts movie. Girls like me don't just end up with the guy they've always wanted." I finish my thought.

"What if..." George stops, as he pulls his breath in. "What if it always should have been us? Do we not owe it to ourselves to find out?"

We do. Of course, we do.

What has been the point of this whole damn experience if we don't? Why else have we been connected this way my whole life if it hasn't been leading to this exact moment? Finally, we are both here. We are here in the same place, at the same time. We are face-to-face and saying the words that have been locked inside of us for forever.

I gently pull him closer. I pull him all the way into the room and swing the door closed behind him. We are so close now that our bodies are touching for the first time. I arch up onto my toes, placing my lips onto his.

George releases my hands, grabbing the small of my back instead. He presses firmly against me teasing my lips with his tongue. My body is ignited. I reach up and run my fingers through his hair giving it a gentle pull. Our lips are locked together as our mouths explore each other. George's fingers run down my hips to the edge of my dress. He glides his hand underneath, caressing the skin on the curve of my legs. I break out in goosebumps from how deliciously ticklish it feels. As he caresses me I unbutton his shirt, pushing it over his shoulders followed by his black t-shirt. His bare chest, muscular and covered with his dark hair draws me in. I want to follow the narrow pattern of hair down past his stomach to where his pants sit. Then slowly, smoothly he lifts my dress up my body and over my head. This is usually the moment I dread the most when I've been with other men for the first time. Naked. The dimples in my pale skin exposed, my belly roll popping out over my thong, all my imperfections on display. But right now, none of those things even matter. I've never felt sexier, more desired in my entire life. I turn around giving him my back. He tenderly kisses my neck as he unhooks my bra letting it drop to the floor with my dress. Reaching around he cups my bare breasts in his hands as he kisses my neck with more passionate ferocity. Our breathing is getting heavier. Our bodies are pulsating. I turn back to face him, looking back into the eyes I've looked into so many times before. George backs me up slowly until I am sitting on the edge of the bed. He slides his jeans down from his waist then carefully climbs over me, on top of me.

Together, after all this time...

I don't want to close my eyes, I don't even want to blink for fear I will open them and find out this has all been just another dream. My nerves are raw edges on top of my skin feeling every movement with such deep intensity. Every touch of his skin on mine sends tingles up and down my spine. His strong fingers gently caress my bare back in small delicate circles. My hand holds firmly onto his shoulder. The curve of his bicep over the top of my arm blocks my view of everything else in the room but him, but I have no need to see anything else. Enveloped in his arms, I never want this feeling to end. I kiss his neck before tucking my head further into his chest. The scent of his body is so familiar, so comforting it feels as though we've been here one hundred times before. Naked, holding each other close, living in a moment of pure happiness.

"I always had a crush on you, my whole life. Did you know?" My voice floats out, barely audible and feeling alien even to myself.

"I knew." He says quickly and kisses the top of my head.

"You didn't!" I playfully slap my hand against his firm chest. "Did you?" I push away slightly to look at him.

"Okay, alright, I confess! I had no idea." His wide smile isn't as convincing as his earnest stare.

"Really?" I ask again.

"Really. I did not know. I always hoped you might. Did you know that I always had a thing for you?" His stare remains fixed on me.

"Don't tease me." I scootch back down into his chest making myself comfortable against his skin.

His hand gently picks up my chin to look at him, "I am not teasing you. I was in awe of you. Your humor, your independence, always thinking, always dreaming. I thought I must have been so boring to you."

I've never seen him this open and vulnerable before in my life.

"How could you be boring to me? You were older and mysterious. You taught me about Ozzy Osbourne. You were like the coolest person I knew." I hold him tighter with every word.

"Were the coolest, past tense?" He raises an eyebrow.

"Are!" I laugh.

"Were?" His fingers run over the sides of my ribs tickling me. My body folds in towards him and out again from the pleasurable pain of it.

"Are! Are, I said, are cool! Past, present and future!" His

hand moves from my ribs to my face. He softly pushes my hair back and kisses me deeply taking my breath away.

"I always thought you would end up with a Backstreet Boy." He says barely removing his lips from mine.

"I was more of an N'SYNC girl," I whisper, locked in the same position.

I tilt my head just slightly so we are kissing again.

"You know what I mean." He says sweetly playing with my hair.

"Well, Justin Timberlake never came knocking." I joked.

"His loss." George's hand runs the length of my back.

"Why didn't you ever tell me how you felt?" I ask, almost afraid to know the answer.

George is quiet, but says softly, "I was afraid."

"Afraid of what?" I push.

"Of your father. The man could intimidate Satan himself." He answers with a small chuckle.

I know he is not being completely forthcoming, masking his meaning in a joke. "Really though?"

"Well, partly. I was afraid of all the stupid things people are afraid of when the heart is involved. Embarrassment, rejection, judgment, sadness. The words that keep us from telling the truth. The feelings that block us, that stop happiness dead in its tracks. In the end, I was afraid of you. That you would never have me." He holds me a little tighter to him.

I reach up and run my fingers along his jawline, feeling his five o" clock shadow as it scratched the skin on my fingertips. "I guess I can't blame you there." I understand exactly where he is coming from.

"So, where are we again?" George opens his arm from around me and turns his body to look out the small hostel room window.

"Barthelona," I say in my best Catalan accent.

"Why on earth did you want to come to Barcelona?" He asks with a nudge.

"Javier Bardem." I quip.

"Who?"

"Antoni Gaudi." I quickly change.

"You are too fast for me." George throws his arm back over me.

"Good!" I laugh as he begins covering my body in kisses.

I can't even believe this moment is real. I try to commit every single second to memory.

"Barcelona, huh?" He kisses my face and gives me a wry smile.

"I owed it to Sami. She wanted to come here. She loves the beach." I say running my hands through his short dark hair.

"The beach that is ten blocks away?" George says sarcastically.

"Well, we're not made of money. We're traveling on a budget, so hotels on the beach are out of the question. But, we don't mind walking."

George pauses for a moment before saying, "I could help with that."

"What do you mean?" I ask confused by his statement...or offer?

"You cannot be happy staying in these hostels and I want to see you happy. How about I get us a proper room somewhere, the best hotel in the city, or something right on the beach if you like. Or at the very least a place with running water." He moves his body back just a tiny bit to look for my reaction.

"This place is not that bad!" I laugh looking around the room. "Are you so posh and European now you've forgotten your roots?" I ask. "We didn't exactly grow up in the lap of luxury."

"How could I ever forget where we came from? I am sorry. I did not mean to be rude. I just want to do something special for you, splurge a little." He says earnestly.

A nice room overlooking the water does sound amazingly romantic, but I can't.

"I won't leave Sami," I say flatly, which he should already know.

"Neither will I. I will get her and her friend a room as well." There is nothing fantastical about his offer. He is completely serious.

"You would do that? A room for Sami and Aaron as well as a room for us?" I ask in disbelief at his generosity.

"Of course I would! Nessa, the past twenty-four hours have been the most unbelievable of my life. I would do anything for you, anything to make you happy." He kisses me again and I can't help the tears coming from my eyes.

"You are amazing. This is more magical than I ever could have dreamed it." I speak slowly as not to completely lose it. George without skipping a single beat wipes away the tears. "But I don't know it feels like too much. We are going home the day after tomorrow, anyway. The trip is basically over."

I still feel quite uncomfortable with such an extravagant gesture. No one has ever wanted to do something so sweet for me, splurge just to make me happy.

As if reading my mind, George says, "Trust me, you deserve it. You, my beautiful Nessa are worth it." I look up at him. "Sami deserves it." He finishes his thought.

"Okay. Let's do it." I excitedly kiss him on his firm full mouth. "I'm sure they are going to be back any minute now." I look over at the clock on the wall. "My god, it's already midnight."

"Maybe they have been having just as much fun as we have," George says giving my bare behind a squeeze.

"I sure hope so," I say just as George rolls me onto my back and leans over to kiss me.

Our hands are everywhere, the sheets are twisted and before I know it the clock on the wall has moved its hands from twelve to one.

Breathless, side by side with our fingers intertwined I have never felt more content in my life. I feel steady. I feel grounded.

"I never expected it would be as perfect as this." George breaks the silence and heavy breathing.

"You thought about this moment?" I ask taken aback.

"I tried not to. I thought it was crazy. But I could not help myself. Crazy or not I could not get you off of my mind." Still holding on to my hand he lifts it up to his mouth to kiss each of my fingers.

I turn over to face him. "I'm familiar with that emotion."

He turns matching me, "Are we crazy?"

"Maybe...well pretty much certainly...What would our parents say if they knew about this?" I asked opening my eyes wide.

He clutches his chest, "I can see it now. Heart attacks all around. Although, my father, my father always adored you. He would be just delighted."

He gently taps my nose with his finger and my heart leaps.

"He has great taste." I wink.

George pulls me closer, runs his fingers through my hair and kisses my eyelids without saying a word. We lay there lost inside our own world.

"Maybe I should come home with you." George murmurs.

In disbelief I look up at him, "Could you even imagine?"

"It would be wonderful." He sings. Pushing his forehead up against mine, "You know what would really throw them over the edge?"

"What?" I retort, my face hurting from smiling so hard.

"Grandchildren."

The word takes my breath away. "You want kids?" I ask exceedingly slowly because I am afraid this might all turn out to be some kind of cruel joke.

George places his hand on my cheek to comfort me. His touch is hypnotizing. "Yes, I want kids. I have always wanted to be a father. Of course, though I will be the bad parent giving them little presents and candies. All the while you are wagging your finger saying I am spoiling them rotten. You, you are the tough parent."

"Me? The tough parent? That's a laugh!"

"How many children do you want?" He questions as he returns to running his fingers through my hair.

"Five!" I say half seriously and half looking to catch his reaction.

"Five?" George's voice raises by a full octave.

"Or one." I squeeze his arm. "I mean being an only child was great for me. I would be happy with just one, but I have this vision of myself as an old woman surrounded by my kids, grandkids, and great-grandkids."

"It is a very romantic vision. That is for certain." George kisses my forehead.

I continue the fantasy. "I've always loved the names Aidan and Isabelle."

"Those are great names, but we will need three more, no?" George dives in with me.

"Hannah, for your mom?" I offer him.

"That is very sweet, but do we have to name one Myrtle after your mom?" He asks with a wince.

"Ah, definitely not. Even she would agree with that. My grandmother's name is Margaret." Hopefully securing name number four.

George smiles, "Maggie is beautiful. Now, how about another boy?"

"Samuel," I answer without a second of hesitation.

"As in Beckett?" George catches my enthusiasm, knowing me all too well.

I bite my lip to hold back my guilty smile. "Maybe..."

"You are such a nerd!" George tickles my sides, taking joy in me squirming beneath him, losing my breath from laughter.

When I catch my breath I hold on tightly to George's chest, "So, how should we tell everyone? It seems a little much for a phone call. I still have some time off when we get back to the states. If you come back with us, we could take a few days and take a road trip to see our parents. It will be a surprise. I know it's sort of tricky and they will certainly be shocked, but like you said... it will be wonderful."

"Wonderful!" He kisses my forehead. I feel like a precious gem.

"Could you really?" I jump, now sitting up next to him with excitement. "Could you really come back with us on Thursday? Or... I mean maybe we could squeeze out another day or two here in Barcelona together first. I'm sure Sami wouldn't object to more time with Aaron, I slide my hand up and down his muscular arm, feeling each soft dark hair under my fingertips as it passes.

George skootches, propping himself up on his elbow and the flat, beige pillow provided by the hostel. He is taking me in completely.

"I'm having one of those moments. One of those moments when you float up from your body and look down at your life and it is unrecognizable. I can't believe I am here with you, so deliriously happy." I gush, feeling as though I might explode with joy.

"Nessa." George pauses contemplatively. "I think we need to have a plan."

"Of course." I try to slow my speech, knowing that my

excitement has my heart racing and my words running. "It doesn't have to be a surprise. I mean we can call them and warn them if you like if you think that would be best."

I honestly don't care how we do it or when we do it. As far as I'm concerned, right now I could stay right here in this room for the rest of my life.

George is quiet again, staring up at the crack in the ceiling that grows from the tiny single pane window on the far wall across to the bathroom door.

"Or maybe, maybe we should just keep this between us for a little while. Just you and I living in this beautiful moment just a little while longer." George says meticulously and not removing his eyes from the ceiling.

"Well, I think Sami and Aaron have a pretty good idea of what is going on here." I laugh.

George, remaining just as still says, "Excluding them obviously. Is Sami good at keeping secrets?"

"The best," I answer without hesitation.

"Then she will keep the secret for us and I do not anticipate Aaron being a problem." George finally turns and faces me.

"I don't follow," I say quietly, not exactly sure what George's plan is yet.

Pushing up off the bed completely George sits next to me, looking into my eyes with the same excitement and nervousness I saw when I met him at the door this evening.

"How about you stay in Europe longer? You can come back to Munich with me. You liked what you saw there, right? Why not work on your writing there, it has such an amazing arts culture. I just know you would be filled with inspiration." He positively sparkles with energy at the idea.

"And what turn tricks for a place to live?" I retort with more indignation than intended, but I can't possibly fathom how that plan would work. I told him I only had enough money to squeeze out the rest of this trip. This dream scenario he is proposing is too unrealistic to be alluring.

"That is the beauty of it. You would not have to worry about money at all." His smile is so wide it must hurt his cheeks to hold it.

"George, I spent all my money coming to Europe in the first place. How could I not worry about it? I have to go back." I really hate being the voice of reason, especially when the idea is so damn enticing.

George grabs my hands in his and holds them tight. "I will take care of everything. All of your living expenses. All you would have to worry about is enjoying the sunshine." He kisses my left cheek, "Leaning a new language." He kisses my right cheek, "And doing what you really want to do with your life." He kisses me on the lips, "You get to write to your heart's content."

I feel paralyzed from the neck down, my body is in shock from what my ears are hearing.

"And us?" I dare to ask.

"And we will not have a pesky ocean keeping us apart anymore." He doesn't move, clearly awaiting my ecstatic reaction.

"That does sound perfect," I say exhaling deeply.

George wraps me up in his arms and as one we slide back down into the bed.

"You and me, sitting out in the sunshine along the Eisbach watching the surfers and sharing a very large, salty pretzel." George weaves the dream scene in bright colors.

"And then what?" I beg for more of the tapestry he is imagining for us.

"And then I whisk you away home because I cannot wait another minute to be with you." He pulls me closer to him.

"And then what?" I plead like a child wanting candy.

"Then you read me your latest brilliant chapter, in the nude, of course." He winks.

"Of course," I respond quite emphatically.

"Nessa, please, please say you will stay." George pushes a stray hair from in front of my face.

"Yes, George, of course, I will stay with you." My eyes well up with joy. Butterflies fill my stomach all the way up to the back of my mouth.

George rolls me onto my back and he is hovering over me. He leans down tenderly kissing my lips before moving onto each eye taking away my happy tears with each kiss he places.

"You are an amazing woman, Nessa Reilly. You deserve every happiness and we are going to be so incredibly happy." George whispers between kisses.

"We...wow! I don't think I'll ever quite get used to hearing that." Looking up into his eyes I can see what he sees. The glow of a future together at last.

And for a moment we are quiet. George's body resting on top of mine. We are silently dreaming together with our eyes wide open, unwilling to lose a single second to sleep. I can no longer feel where my body ends and his begins.

"Do you want to live in Munich forever, I mean don't you miss your family?" I asked dreamily, thinking of all the places our future together could lead us.

"No, I do not want to stay in Munich forever. But I am not dying to move back to Philadelphia either." He says with a small chuckle at the end.

"No one is dying to go back to Philadelphia." I follow up slyly. "But I mean sometime soon we would go back, right? Maybe eat that very large, salty pretzel in Rittenhouse Square or down the shore somewhere." I gently push, knowing I don't want to be so far from my family and friends if we are planning on having children.

"Of course we will, eventually. That sounds simply amazing. There are just a lot of things I have to consider, that I have to take care of. I have a wife and a life in Germany." He says so nonchalantly it sucks the oxygen from my lungs.

"A wife," I repeat to know I heard him correctly.

"Yes?" He says with a confused inflection in his voice.

"Greta," I confirm what I already know to be true.

"Yes." He says more sternly this time, clearly marking his confusion with my line of questioning.

"You haven't left her?" The question cuts my mouth as I say it.

George pauses for a moment, "Nessa, this is not something I planned in advance. How could I know this would happen when I arrived here? I had hoped, but I never knew you would feel the same way I do."

"But you are going to leave her? When you get back to Munich?" I feel my heart beating in my throat.

"We, when we get back to Munich." He says with the same sweet sincerity he had when painting the vision of us together.

"You will leave her then though, right?" I continue on.

"No. It is not that easy. I cannot snap my fingers and it is done. If I could I would do it right this second, but there are a lot of details to consider that you are not seeing right now. But I can be married and nothing would change between us." He tries to pull me close but I feel as stiff as a wooden board against him.

I push myself up and sit on the edge of the bed turning my back towards him. "Where does she think you are right now?" The full weight of what we have just done suddenly landing upon my shoulders.

"Called out of town for work, why?" I feel George sit up in the bed.

"And she believes that?" I ask feeling incredibly small, pushed into the floor by gravity and guilt.

"It happens quite a lot." George puts his hand on my shoulder, but I pull away.

"Does it, really?" I stand up and turn around to look at him. "Or does this happen quite a lot and you call it work?" I can't help myself from asking the questions I don't really want the answers to, so I spit them out like venom.

"Nessa." George is up on his knees on top of the bed. "Nessa, you are spiraling. Do you want the truth?" He holds out his hands to me.

"Yes," I demand, unwilling to accept his gesture of intimacy.

"I have never been unfaithful to Greta. Not once. I have never even considered it. Not until last night, not until I saw your face again. Not until I felt you in my arms and knew I did not want to let you go. I could not let you go again. I thought I was happily married, but I had forgotten what happy really feels like." George pauses and reaches his hand out to me again. "Do you believe me?"

He looks like a sad puppy dog kneeling on the bed before me. I take his hands because I can honestly say, "I do."

"Tell me you feel the same. Tell me I am not alone here. Is this not what you wanted too?" The emotion and fear rumble in his voice.

I kneel onto the bed with him, "You have no idea how much."

"Then why would we throw it all away?" His hands slide up my arms and around my shoulders to hold me tight. "Why, when we have finally found each other would we choose to walk away?"

"I... I don't know." My head is spinning.

"Then this seems obvious," George says unwavering in his confidence.

The butterflies in my stomach have turned into bees, rumbling, buzzing and flying into the walls.

"You want me to move to Munich with you?" I ask, still unable to believe my life right now.

"Yes," George confirms, but his answer doesn't make me feel any more confident about the plan at hand. My excitement and fear are inseparably blended together.

"And you would pay for me to live there just so you could see me? I could spend my days writing and my nights like this?" I can start to see it so clearly, more clearly than any of my dreams ever predicted.

"Yes, yes, please say you will." He is pleading with me. I have never seen this side of George before. He is completely open and exposed.

I can't seem to manage to make any words. My mouth is open and my eyes are focused on George, but I can't seem to speak. There are a million things I want to say and even more, I need to say.

George bends his knees and we both lower back down to sitting on the bed. Side by side with our backs against the headboard in silence until the scream of an ambulance siren startles us both into laughter.

"Nessa, come home with me," George says as soft as a prayer.

"But you won't divorce your wife if I do." The words scald my mouth as they slowly pour out.

"Yes." My eyes well at George's answer. "No, I mean yes at some point, yes I will file for divorce." He pauses, "But no, not right away."

"When?" I jump. Demanding an answer faster than he is clearly willing or able to give.

"I cannot give you a date and time right this second, Nessa. It is bigger than us, but that does not change what we have. Life is not all black and white it is full of colors. This is simply our color, our beautiful color. Can you see that?" He asks with the same pleading tone in his voice as before but now with a distinct piqued undertone.

Wrapping his arm around me, George slides us back down the bed and suddenly we are cuddled together. I hold on to his strong body like a koala bear on a Eucalyptus tree.

"This could be us." I sigh, the warmth of his body relaxing every tense muscle in my body.

"This could be us." He strokes my arms with his fingertips.

"And we would be together, for real." I look up into his eyes and they are so full of love.

"This is as real as it gets." He whispers into my ear.

"Do you...love me?" The bees trapped inside me buzz more ferociously at the question I've asked.

And without hesitation, George says, "I think I have always loved you."

"You are saying all the right things." Though I feel like I might be sick.

"Believe me. Nessa, I love you and I want to be with you... Do you feel the same?" My heart stops at the question. I am no longer dreaming. George is flesh and blood here before me. He is naked, holding me tight in bed proclaiming his love for me. It is all I have ever wanted for as long as I can remember, but it's not at all the same.

"Nessa?" George gives me a little nudge, as I have clearly been staring off into the distance walking the halls of my own mind.

"I..." I look him straight in the eyes. The pain inside me is almost too much to bear, but I can't stop the truth from coming out of my mouth, "I don't...George, I don't."

Then we are still and silent. We both close our eyes. Sleep finally comes to us. And I do not dream.

CHAPTER 15
GOTHIC ROMANCE

I just can't help smiling. Smiling and giggling like a small child. That's how happy I feel. Aaron's painfully uncoordinated salsa down the stairs followed by nearly dropping the bag of cherries and bottle of wine in front of the desk manager has me in a complete fit of laughter.

"The look on his face!" I squeeze out, barely able to breathe at this point.

"I think he quite enjoyed it. I may have a future as a busker here along Las Ramblas." He laughs back at me. As we pass through the front door of the hostel, he completes his thought with another quick step back throwing his hip out and bumping me. "Come now, I'm going to need a partner out there. I know you've got a little dance in yah." He teases me.

"No. I am not a dancer. Headbanging yes, that I can do. Dancing though, it's all very spazzy. Arms and legs flying everywhere. That's a big NO!" I assert grabbing the bottle of wine from his arms.

The night is super humid. Walking out of our barely standing hostel into the street feels like walking into a massive sheet of fly paper. Luckily we are only lit by the light of the moon, the warm glow of round street lights and a few neon signs that speckle the street. It gives the heat a more romantic essence and masks the tiny beads of sweat forming around my temples. Even though we are just a few alleys deep into the Gothic Quarter from the busy Las Ramblas, it feels like we are in our own little world. There are a few people taking a late evening stroll. A family is in line a few feet away at the Churros stand that is giving off the most heavenly scent of sugar. The bar right next door is glowing with candle-light and quiet conversation. Peeking through the window you can see it is dark and atmospheric inside. But the cobble-stone streets really make you believe you have wandered into another century. I am swept up in this enigmatic place, a place that feels alive with magic, both light, and dark.

I realize I've been standing just outside the hostel door for some time now just looking, watching, and inspecting everything I can see from this spot. I don't want to miss anything, I want to be taking in everything the city offers.

Aaron is only a few steps ahead of me. He has turned back, watching me watching the world.

"You are very special, Sami, you know that, right?" He asks softly, approaching me.

"What do you mean?" My full attention now turned to him.

"You see things. You're an observer. What others would pass by, you take in." His eyes are burning straight into my soul.

"No one has ever described me like that before. I hope it's a good thing." I say, suddenly feeling shy like I've been found doing something I wasn't supposed to be doing.

Aaron steps forward reaching out for my hand and I give it to him. He leads me forward as he steps back to the bench behind him.

"It's a very good thing. You are the most interesting person I've ever met." He releases my hand as we both sit on the bench.

It is the perfect spot facing the hostel entrance so we can enjoy the cool wafts of air conditioning coming from its permanently opened front door as we watch for Nessa or George, or Nessa and George. But it's shadowed enough from the fluorescent glow to be private and just for us.

"Well pop her open already." Aaron leans into me, motioning toward the bottle of wine still sealed up in my hand.

I twist the aluminum cap in my hand until it breaks, "Classy," I wink at him before tipping the bottle up to my lips. The dark red wine is sweet with the taste of cinnamon, oranges, and apples. Even though the liquid feels cool as I drink it down, I immediately feel the warming effects in my body. I must have seriously lost my buzz when George showed up.

"Now that was classy." Aaron laughs.

I hand the bottle to him and he instinctively hands me the bag of cherries in return.

"Two peas in a pod." He says tipping the bottle up to his own mouth and following suit. "What are you thinking about?" He asks, reading my falling face with the skill of someone who has known me for much longer than twenty-four hours.

"I'm feeling sort of guilty," I confess.

"Nessa?" He asks, clearly already knowing the answer.

I shake my head affirmatively as he hands me back the bottle for a sip.

"I'm worried about her. I have this sinking feeling that whatever is being said or done between them..." I pause trying to find the words that match my emotions, "She will be the one hurt or end up sad or broken. And here I am, at this moment, so genuinely happy and filled with excitement at the prospect of each moment to come."

My head is tilted down toward the bottle of wine in my hand, but I lift my eyes ever so slightly to catch his reaction to what I've said. His eyes are there, right there waiting for me to look up. Warm and round, a deep chocolate brown they welcome me in. No judgment or dismissal. I hand him back the wine.

"Now if there's one thing I've learnt in meeting the two of you." He pauses briefly to wrap his arm around my shoulders. "I don't think Nessa nor you my sweet, saucy Sami could ever be broken. Sad yes, maybe. Hurt, it's a part of life. But never ever broken. You are both incredibly bright, willful and shall always land on your feet. Plus, you have each other. What you've got there is much more powerful stuff than anything any bloke could muster."

Our bodies are pressed up into each other side by side, my shoulder under his arm. I can't really see his face though, so I pull my legs up one at a time and place them over his. My knees now resting on his thighs, I turn inward to face him. "I don't know why I met you, why I walked into your bar, or why I struck up a conversation with you when all I wanted was to wallow in my own solitude, but I'm sure glad I did."

Leaning his forehead in to meet mine, he places it there a moment and says, "I'm absolutely delighted you did."

Is this the moment? I wonder. Is he going to kiss me? We are so close, watching each other so carefully. I've thought about this moment since he arrived earlier this evening. As soon as I saw him again all these feelings came rushing into my body, my brain, my heart. But he doesn't kiss me. He pulls his head back and hands me the bottle of Sangria. I take one sip from the quickly emptying bottle and then I take another.

"It might be a long night out here waiting for them." I wink and hand him back the bottle which he takes gladly.

"Well, if I am going to stay here with you on this bench all night, and I'm not saying I'm going to." He coyly teases me.

"Go on," I say.

"I think we should get to know each other better." He continues.

I pop a cherry off its stem into my mouth, "Do you propose a game?"

"I do indeed." His voice full of satisfaction at his own cleverness. "It's called unpopular opinions and we play by sharing our most unpopular opinions on anything from food to music, pop culture to politics, family, life, what have you."

"How do you win?" I ask intently.

"You Americans, always so competitive." He jostles my legs, still resting comfortably upon him. "We both win, how's that sound?"

"I accept your terms." I cock my head to the side and pop another delicious cherry into my mouth.

He flashes a devilish smile and takes a cherry for himself from the bag. "Let's start off easy shall we?"

"That will be a fun change for us." I quickly retort.

"Let's start with food. Unpopular opinion, I do not enjoy sweets. Candies, cakes, ice cream, none of it. Give me savory every day of the week, thank you." He raises one eyebrow, clearly searching my face for a disgusted reaction.

"Good, more for me then." I match my eyebrow to his. "Alright, unpopular opinion, I don't like cheese. I'll have it on some pizza fine, but that's about it." I reach my hand out for the bottle of Sangria and he gladly concedes it. I don't know if it is this moment we are in, or if it is just being in Spain, but it is the best tasting Sangria I have ever had. The sip I take fills me with such delight.

"Alright now, movies. Unpopular opinion, The Godfather is rubbish." Aaron states with complete confidence.

I think for a moment, "Unpopular opinion," I follow with,

"Pretty Woman is terrible, not even the slightest bit romantic to me. It literally makes me cringe when I pass by it changing the channels."

"Do you like the game so far?" Aaron asks me so thoughtfully.

"Very much." I lean nearly touching my face to his to answer.

"Shall we try a harder topic?" He continues his line of questioning leading us through the game.

I shake my head up and down as I take down more from the bottle.

"I've a feeling this will be a real hot button topic for you. Music." Our eyes simultaneously widen in the most cartoonish way and I burst out laughing.

"I'll go first this time" I start, "Unpopular opinion, I hate Billy Joel."

Aaron stops as he was just about to grab another cherry his mouth agape. "The piano man? Really?" He asks before continuing on into the open bag on my lap.

"Well, yea I was never much of a fan, to begin with. Then in high school, I was dating this guy. His dad was obsessed with Billy Joel. He was also a pretty sloppy drunk too. Well, any night I'd be over at the house, his dad would be drunk off his ass and blaring Billy Joel in the living room. Singing along like his life depended on it. Some nights his mom would go out back and flip the breaker to turn all the electric off to the house until he passed out. We would just sit in the dark waiting for him to pass out." I realize I have gone on a total tangent. "So, yea. No Billy Joel for me."

"Wow! That's a pretty extreme experience to have gone through at a young age. No wonder you can't stand Billy Joel. Mine feels a bit silly now. But, unpopular opinion, I don't get the appeal of KISS. The whole getup, I can't get around it to even really hear the music."

"You don't want to rock and roll all night and party every day?" I ask as seriously as I possibly can, with nearly half the bottle of Sangria in me.

Aaron takes a drink and quite animatedly continues, "See now, no I do not want to rock and roll all night and party every day, not if it means I've got to have my face all painted up. And, don't even get me started on the Spandex." He waves down toward his body. "Not a good look."

"I don't think wearing the makeup and spandex is a prerequisite for fandom, but I get it. It is very polarizing. They also went through a very dark period when they started making disco music. You don't need that in your life." I hand him the bottle of wine and he immediately takes a long sip.

"Ok." I continue, "Mr. Literature degree. Unpopular opinion, I don't like The Great Gatsby. There is nothing redeemable about any of the characters. I could care less about them."

He squints his eyes at me for a moment and I feel a tingle of anticipation at what he might be about to say.

"Unpopular opinion, well not opinion per se, but you'll cop on. I have never read nor seen any of the Harry Potter series." He is completely still, staring at me.

"But how? You're English." I don't understand.

"I just never did, I was a bit on the older side when it all started, so my mates weren't into it. I never took the time to go back." He's almost embarrassed.

"I didn't think there was anyone our age who hadn't read or at least seen Harry Potter. Oh my god!" I yell in excitement at my next thought. I grasp his arm and plead, "Can we have a Harry Potter marathon? We will watch all of the movies back to back. We can easily do it in a weekend."

He smiles back at me so warmly, but in a sad whisper reminds me, "We don't have a weekend though, do we? You'll be gone day after next. Then who knows if-"

I stop him, "Then we will watch together over Skype, televisions synced and laptops open." I can't stand the thought of us saying goodbye.

Aaron is lightly running his thumb up and down on my leg, "You know, I think you did win this game after all."

"Is it over, can't we have one more?" I ask while digging into the nearly empty cherry bag. Thank goodness there is a backup.

"A bonus round, eh?" Aaron concedes. "Let's make it a wild card. Life in general."

"I like it. Let me think for a moment." I search my mind as my eyes wander around the place where we are sitting. I can see he is doing the same.

Without taking my eyes off the flickering candlelight in the bar window across the way I start, "Unpopular opinion, I don't want to have kids." I immediately feel exposed in front of him. I don't know why it came out of my mouth. I've felt this way for a while now, but I've never told a soul until this moment. Maybe it's the wine or the night or the game or just him. "I'm not really sure why I've just said that." I may have just ruined everything.

"Is it true, what you've said?" He asks slowly.

"Yes. I have never felt what other women feel. That urge to be a mother, the desire to carry a baby. I don't have it. I wish I could feel it just for a day just to know what it was like. Sometimes, I think I must be deficient somehow. Defective. I believe Charles Darwin would certainly want to talk to me about it." I trail off still feeling slightly embarrassed.

"Well, despite what you may have heard necromancy isn't taught in English schools, so I shan't be inviting Charles Darwin to this bench anytime this evening." His humor erases my self-consciousness. "Sami, you're secret is safe with me if that's how you like it. But I think you're exceedingly clever to know your own feelings and not just follow along with the production line as it were. My mother wasn't a very warm, nurturing woman. Don't think she much wanted to be a mother but became one nevertheless. It would've been better had she sorted that out sooner." Aaron says solemnly. His normally sweet expression has dropped into something more serious and the sight of it pulls deeply at my heart-strings.

"I'm sorry, she must have been young when she passed," I say quietly, not really sure what to say.

"She's not passed, just passed on me. I was about ten when she took off. But my dad is the tops, really. He's the one who raised me. He's my best mate." The smile has returned somewhat to his face.

"That's beautiful, the relationship you have with your dad." I gently place my hand over his while offering him a cherry from the bag.

He happily accepts, "I guess this got a bit deeper than say the Zoo Game, huh?"

"Not a very high bar." I divulge, "But I've enjoyed it, I like talking with you. Even about the deep stuff. It's easy."

He gives my calf a light squeeze and hands me back the bottle. "Go on. Finish her off."

And so I do, the length of the sip is a little more than ladylike, but we are definitely past the point of that being embarrassing. I gaze up at the hostel's second-floor window. The window that opens up to the hallway where our room is located. The light looks dim and there is no hint of movement.

"I think we might be here for a while longer." I uninten-tionally apologize. "It is absolutely still up there."

"If we have to sit here until morning comes, I wouldn't be bothered one bit." Aaron reaches his long, but muscular arm around me and pulls me in even closer until I'm folded up into the fetal position over his legs. He is warm and smells like the sweet, but spicy body wash I used in his shower. We sit like that, curled into each other until the street is bare and we are the only people left. It feels like it could be the end of the world, no one left but us. And that would be perfectly fine. We alternate between boisterous, rapid-fire conversation and long, comfortable silences. The bar's candles have all been blown out. Some couples left hand in hand, others attached by the mouth and even in Spain girl's night out ends with ladies walking arm in arm laughing into the night. There is a warm breeze blowing through the trees above us. Even though, I couldn't be further from bored my body is tired and lets out a massive yawn. Aaron watches me just before yawning himself.

"You're tired" I roll my head to look up into his eyes.

"You started it." He squeezes my hand. "How about we go upstairs? No funny business!" He contorts his eyebrows. "You can sleep in my room and we'll slip a note under the door for Nessa. That way she knows where to find you."

Sleep does sound amazing right now. "I'm guessing they must have fallen asleep themselves."

"Or they're otherwise occupied" Aaron laughs. "Come on." He taps my legs to move.

Slowly, very slowly I lift my legs off his lap and for the first time in hours my feet touch the ground. It's foreign and unenjoyable, to say the least. Aaron's arm doesn't leave me once as we stand up. Moving as one we make our way into the hostel wincing as the lights burn our eyes that have become accustomed to the dark. The steps up to the second floor feel like a dozen mini mountains, but we are finally at the door to Aaron's room.

"Wait there, he stops me from walking in. He comes back with a piece of notebook paper and a pen.

"How shall we say it?" He asks ready to scribe.

"Just put, staying in Aaron's room. Come knock when

you're up. Love- S." I watch as he scribbles away before quickly placing it under the second door to the left.

"Can you hear anything?" I whisper.

He gingerly places his ear to the door listening for several seconds but shakes his head.

"Not a thing." He returns to where I have propped myself in the doorway.

"I hope she's alright." I wrap my arms around his waist for a hug.

His arms wrapped around my shoulders as he starts to walk me sideways into the room.

"Come on little penguin, time to sleep. Nothing more you can do tonight." He says into my ear.

I giggle at the funny walk and hold him tighter. "Little penguin, I like that."

He sits me down on the bed and returns to close the door. I slip under the thin cream colored sheet, not even bothering to take off my clothes. My eyes so heavy they start to close.

"Sleep tight, little penguin," Aaron says turning off the light.

I open up my eyes to see him laying a blanket on the floor. "Aren't you getting in?"

"Yea, uh yes. Of course. If you'd have me." Aaron jumps up from the floor and lays the blanket over my legs.

"Yes, I'd definitely have you." I lean back to look at him over my shoulder

He unbuttons his shirt revealing a gray tank top before crawling under the covers with me.

"Good night, big penguin." I coo.

And with that, he lays his arm over the top of me keeping me close for the rest of the night.

CHAPTER 16
THE COLLAPSE

There is no alarm sounding, no one pounding on the door in search of us. The sun didn't even greet the dawn of a new day. There is nothing remotely spectacular about waking up this morning, but it is a day I will remember down to my bones for the rest of my life. Gray rain is dripping slowly outside of the window. It casts a shadow over every item in the room, including us. There is no sound coming up from the street below. The only sound is that of muffled voices and the creaking floorboards of the hostel that permeate this tiny unassuming room. If I listed off a description of the places I thought my life would change forever, this scene would be foreign to it. We are both awake. I can feel it, but I'm afraid to open my eyes and know it. So I lay here holding him as tightly as I can and feel his arms around me in return. I want to remember everything, even the pain I feel in my chest. I inhale deeply, taking in the salt smell of his sand tone skin. I don't know how long we've slept for, but we haven't moved a muscle from where we both closed our eyes for the first time. I take account of my body all the way from my toes to my hair. I absorb the feeling of where his body touches mine. Every hair tickling the skin on my legs, the curve of his thigh over mine, the weight of his arm that makes me feel as safe as a swaddled newborn, and the warmth of his breath over my ear. I wish we could stay here in this moment, exist in a vacuum of time and space where nothing before or after ever exists. But it cannot be.

Gently, slowly I feel George's strong fingers move up from their home on my shoulder and sweetly sweep the hair back from my face. I break completely. My body still, the tears run from the eyes I have yet had the power to open. George doesn't say a word, he just continues to brush my hair back. The repetition is soft and soothing like a wave crashing upon the shore. After a few minutes, he leans his head down ever so slightly, places his lips on my forehead and allows them to rest there. Breathing feels strange, like a distant memory and I can't fight it any longer. I open my tear filled eyes to see the same lines traveling down George's cheeks from his own blurred eyes. I lean my head back to look at him fully and bring my hand up to hold his face in my palm. I try to wipe his tears with my thumb, but more come to replace each one. We share a kiss. It is soft, full, and wet with salt water tears. Everything we want to say to each other is there in that kiss, all of the love, sadness, gratitude, and longing rolled up into ten seconds of the purest connection I've ever felt. Together we lay without saying a word for what only feels like minutes, but I know must be hours. Him hoping I will change my mind, me hoping I will change my heart.

The moments that follow are a blur. We start to move, very slowly at first like we are removing dirt from a fossil, fearing breaking it completely. We get dressed, not bothering to shower first and as I slip my top over my head I turn to see George standing by the door. He is just inches from where he begged me to come in hours before, the place where he told me it was always supposed to be us. The moment we have both been fighting from existing has arrived.

"Time for me to go." He says, half asking and half stating the facts.

I cross the room and throw my arms around his neck.

"Nessa." His arms wrap around my lower back pulling me close, "I love you. That will never change. "

I dig my head into his chest, "I love you too. It's just not the right time for us, it has never been the right time."

George picks my chin up with his finger and kisses me. One last kiss.

"Maybe, not the right time just means not the right person. He will find you, Nessa. And there won't be any questions of time."

And with that George opens the door to the hostel hallway and walks away. The orange glow from the lights assaults my fragile eyes. But at the end of the hall before reaching the stairs, he turns back to look at me one last time. His lips curl into a smile and he winks. Involuntarily, the right side of my mouth lifts into a smile and then he is gone.

CHAPTER 17

THIRTY-SIX HOURS

Opening my eyes to this dim morning and drab room feels something strangely akin to opening my eyes on the first day of summer vacation as a child. The day could hold any adventure and many treasures to behold. The joy of freedom is sewn into its very fabric. Aaron's long, ink covered arm is still around me keeping me safe and warm. I turn underneath it so I can face him. His kind, dark eyes are still shut under his heavy blanket of black eyebrows. I watch his chest rise and fall with each deep breath. I can't help but smile. As I lay here looking at this man I've known for thirty-six hours I feel love and appreciation that whatever power up above brought us together for whatever amount of time we have. Without thinking, I close my eyes, tilt my head up and kiss him tenderly on the mouth. I pull back and open my eyes expecting to see him still sleeping so serenely, but instead, Aaron's eyes are wide open watching me. He doesn't say anything and a sudden panic comes over me.

"I'm sorry. I just wanted." But before I can stutter out another syllable he leans into me. His arm moves from casually slung over my body to purposefully holding me, his hand spread wide between my shoulder blades. And he kisses me. A firm, meaningful kiss. My stomach flips over and over again with excitement. My body reacting instinctually to the moment, I crawl further toward him so that now we are pressed together.

Our bodies begin moving in time to the sound of the rain outside, writhing to the water's rhythm. My leg slips over his hip until my dress is scrunched all the way up to my ribs. "You have the most perfect bum." He grabs hold of me, giving my cheeks a sturdy squeeze. His face is in my neck while I quickly unbutton his jeans. Our connection is electric and unlike anything I've ever experienced before in my life. Aaron lifts me over so I am on top of him, straddling his waist. He pulls my dress over my head and tosses it to the side of the bed. I rock back and forth on top of him unclipping my bra at the same time. His face flushed and his eyes round at the sight of me. I didn't believe a man like him existed.

Completely breathless, completely naked and completely content, we lay there in the world's smallest bed listening to the wind outside.

"Sami," Aaron says softly, breaking the silence. "You know I have to go back to Berlin today. I can't dodge my classes tomorrow."

"I know." We are clearly both saddened by the glaring truth that our time together is almost over.

"But, maybe I could come to visit you during the Christmas holiday?" He added with trepidation

"Really?" I perk up at the thought.

"If it puts a smile like that on your face, then yes, of course, I could. Would you show me around your nation's capital?" He grins ear to ear.

"Yes, yes, yes, of course, I would! I kiss him excitedly.

Knock. Knock.

A small barely audible rapping comes from the hostel door.

"Sami..."

Nessa's voice is weak and her sadness is palpable in just a single word from her mouth.

I quickly pull my dress back on over my head and run for the door. I barely have it open before Nessa collapses into my arms a mess of hair and tears.

"It's over" She whispers.

EPILOGUE
THE NEXT CHAPTER

"Yes, I'm here, finally!" I turn down the radio with my right hand. "That last stretch from Georgia took for fucking ever!"

I clench the phone between my shoulder and ear as I put the car into park.

"No, it is certainly not cool down here."

My eyes narrow under my sunglasses as I look up at the white and cinnamon, Spanish style apartment building. It sparkles in the September sun.

"Sami, can I call you back once I get inside and get settled? Ok...yes...I love you too. Bye."

I drove eight hundred and fifty miles from Washington D.C. to Orlando, Florida in just over a day. I stopped for a few hours to sleep in South Carolina when I felt I just couldn't keep my eyes open any longer.

Today marks ten whole days since George and I said our goodbyes in that tiny hostel in the middle of Barcelona. I never used to understand when people would talk about broken hearts. Intellectually, I could grasp the ideas of sadness and loss. I would nod my head in sympathy without ever fully knowing. My heart had always been so full, it was overflowing with yearning and hope. I didn't understand how when a heart cracks open all of that deep feeling pours out. It invades the body's other organs. It curdles the stomach, weakens the muscles, tires the bones, and tightens the chest to the point you can barely breathe. Finally, all of the over-flowing emotions sinks down into the feet and you are locked to the floor unable to lift the cement shoes that your own necrotizing passion has created. That morning in Spain, my heart broke.

George disappeared from my sight. Absolutely frozen, I counted to twenty. In my mind that seemed like all the time, it would take for him to leave the building...fifteen, sixteen, seventeen, eighteen, nineteen, twenty.

I knew I wasn't going to make it, that I couldn't keep the brave face on any longer so I hobbled over to Aaron's door praying Sami would be there. The five steps were exhausting. I leaned up on the door and knocked. "Sami?"

Before I can even knock a second time, Sami swings the door open into the room.

She looks beautiful and happy, but all I can squeeze out is "It's over."

And with that, I collapsed like a ragdoll. My limbs bent up underneath me and I sank into the hard wooden floor, only slightly propped up by the splintered door frame. Fully realizing the disgusting display I was creating, I was grateful that Sami and Aaron quickly came to my rescue. Not even a minute on the floor before sweet Sami's beautiful blonde hair and freckles appeared in front of me. Down on the floor, curled next to me, holding me with all her strength. I hear, but do not fully comprehend what she is telling Aaron until he bends down to pick me off the floor and carries me into the room placing me carefully on the bed. Sitting on the creaking wooden rocking chair in the corner of their room,

Sami and Aaron both watch me like new parents with a newborn baby. The shock of it all fades slowly as I lie there curled in the fetal position. There is only one thing on my mind, one thing that keeps repeating over in my head until my voice is strong enough to speak it out loud, "I want to go home."

My motor skills fully returned by the time Sami booked our tickets back to the states. She amazingly packed everything while I showered in Aaron's room so I wouldn't have to go back to ours. Sami and I both shed tears during the drive to the airport. Her goodbye to Aaron at his gate is solemn but tender and full of hope.

It wasn't until we were over halfway across the Atlantic that I had a moment of revelation. We were not far off the coast of Canada, just around where I imagine the Titanic sank and I could still taste his breath on my lips. I peered out the window. Sami's sleeping head nestled into my shoulder I stared down into the perfect blue water and smiled at its serene beauty. That's when I realized there is way too much beauty in this world to see and experience that I've missed because I was so caught up in the idea of my own fate. I was waiting for the beauty to present itself to me, waiting for the perfect moment, waiting to live. I don't want to wait anymore.

At that moment, for the first time since I saw him on that cold December night more than twenty years ago, I felt free. My eyes didn't start to tear at the memory because it no longer plays out like the beginning of a cartoon love story.

I decided that I need to make a complete change. I need to take a risk. No more pulling pints and serving up half-price appetizers to assholes who could easily pay full price and tip a full twenty percent.

And, so, when I touched back down in Washington, D.C. I made quick work of it. I found a sublet for the lease on my place, picked a sunny location and put a deposit on a new apartment. I packed what I could fit into my car and hit the road.

The red string of fate that always had me tethered to a false belief in love has snapped. It couldn't withstand the pressure test George and I put it through. Or perhaps this is what the string was always meant to do. It was meant to lead me into this new phase of my life. George will always be a part of me, the part that has made me who I am today. But he is not part of who I will be someday. He is not my tomorrow. I am my tomorrow.

I am ready for the next chapter.

A new state, a new life, and most importantly a new Nessa.

Oh...and... I am writing it all down.

The End

ABOUT THE AUTHOR

Amanda is a brand new author with this being her first foray into the world of novel writing. Having spent the past ten years as a playwright, she is ready to bring her characters off of the stage, on to the page and into your hands.

Holding a Masters of Philosophy in Theatre and Performance with a focus on playwriting from Trinity College Dublin, Amanda's work has been published and produced both in the United States and Internationally.

Traveling the world and working in the entertainment industry has gifted her with quite the collection of adventurous, provocative, funny and outrageous stories to share. But more than anything she writes about real women with real bodies, real flaws, real dreams and real loves.

Her writing, like herself, will always contain quippy humor, heart, feminism, music lyrics, pop culture references and of course...coffee.

Keep in touch
www.Amandascheirer.com

Made in the USA
Lexington, KY
17 November 2019